THE HOUSEMATES

AN EXTREME HORROR NOVEL

IAIN ROB WRIGHT

ULCERATED PRESS

Dedicated to my wife
for all that she goes through.

"All that is necessary for the triumph of evil is for good men to do nothing."

– **Edmund Burke.**

"Competition is a sin."

– **John D. Rockefeller**

"Game Over."

– **Jigsaw,** *Saw* **(2004)**

DAY 1

The ferry glided ashore. A bus waited on the hill. Rain came down in silver sheets against the velvet darkness of the endless night.

Damien didn't like wearing the hood over his head and had managed to peek out from beneath it several times in the last hour. It was uncomfortable being in the dark, unable to see, unable to even hear properly.

Damien's hosts had told him that the hood was necessary – that the location of the island must be kept secret. The only information they had divulged willingly was that his destination was somewhere off the northern coast of Scotland. The atmosphere's cold, penetrating bite made it easy to believe that Damien had been taken north. He rubbed at his shoulders.

Freezing my bloody knob off here.

Not wanting to push his luck, Damien pulled the hood back down over his face and listened intently. It sounded like the captain of the small passenger ferry was about to give orders.

"Okay, everybody! I'm afraid you will have to leave your

hoods on for just a little while longer. The house is just over a mile inland. A bus will take you there now, and then you can finally take the hoods off and settle in."

There were sighs of relief from all around. Damien wasn't sure how many other people were on the ferry with him, but he estimated at least ten – definitely enough bodies to constitute a crowd. They were all wearing hoods the same as his.

So I have about a dozen competitors. That puts my odds of winning pretty low.

Near the ferry's bow, a man had begun ushering everybody ashore, barking orders in a clipped tone like machine gun fire. Damien stumbled past the gruff gentleman and was hustled along onto what felt beneath his feet like a wooden jetty. The freezing rain made him shudder as he left the shelter of the boat.

Remind me never to come to Scotland again if this is what it's like.

Damien started up an incline, towards where he imagined the bus was parked. An engine idled nearby and the acrid odour of spent petrol mingled with the scent of wet soil. An owl hooted.

When Damien finally stepped onto the waiting bus, he greeted the heavenly warmth with glee. It must have been several hours since his journey had begun and he was starting to feel the weariness in his bones.

Damien's hosts had collected him from a train station in Sheffield, where he had then been driven even further north for almost three hours. That was when he had been told to put the hood on. He was ushered onto a waiting coach with several other people and then continued on yet another leg of the journey, which had ended with the trip on the ferry from which he had just departed.

The hood prevented Damien from seeing who his companions were on the bus, but he heard some of them chatting blindly up ahead as he navigated the aisle.

Time became a blur. Weariness and boredom had led to a dazed passing of seconds and minutes and hours until Damien felt nothing but the desire to sleep. He was glad to hear he was now only a mile away from his final destination.

Thought I'd never bloody get there.

He groped his way along the aisle of the stationary bus and found himself a seat on the left. He sat down and relaxed back into the soft cushion.

Oh, yeah. That feels better. My arse is killing me.

Just another twenty minutes and this wretched trip will be over.

Nerves began to tickle at Damien's psyche as he sat there and waited for the bus to get moving. The bizarre nature of the situation began to sink in. Home seemed far away; he already missed his friends, his work, his old life. It was a situation he never would have got himself into usually, but...

When needs must...

The Devil drives.

Damien felt someone dump down on the seat behind him. The bus grumbled into gear and started moving. The rain continued falling heavy, thudding against the window panels on both sides.

Damien closed his eyes beneath his hood and allowed himself to rest. He was worried that rest would be hard to come by during the days ahead.

The bus sped up, jerking and hopping as it traversed uneven terrain. A couple of times it felt as though the vehicle had gone off road completely. There were no sounds coming from outside, no noise from other traffic, no grinding steel of industrial buildings. Wherever the bus was heading, it was seemingly in the middle of nowhere.

The stranger who had sat on the seat behind Damien leant forward and whispered. "Pretty exciting, huh?"

With the hood still over his head, Damien was unsure if the woman's question had been directed at him. After a few seconds he decided that it was and gave a reply. "I don't know if 'exciting' is the word I would use."

"Really, then how would you describe it?"

"Overdone."

"What do you mean?"

"I mean this is all a bit dramatic. We've been whisked away in the dead of night under the cover of darkness to a destination we know nothing about. Is it really necessary?"

"It's just part of the experience. Putting on a good show."

"It's stupid." Damien sighed. He pulled the hood off his head and blinked his eyes. He'd had enough of being in the dark. It was ridiculous. He understood the need for privacy, to a certain extent, but he was done feeling like a prisoner of war.

"Sir, please put your hood back on!"

Damien glanced down the aisle to see that the bus driver was twisting around. The man was skeletal with cheekbones that leapt out at right-angles. Beside him stood a colleague, a burly man in a set of black overalls and work boots.

"Sir," said the burly man beside the driver. His dark eyes had narrowed and were targeted at Damien like rifle sights. "Put your hood back on or you will be disqualified. You must obey the rules at all times. That is what you agreed when you signed up for the show."

Damien took a second to gaze out of the rain-soaked window. A flash of lightning lit up the sky and the landscape came briefly into view. The entire area was marked by grassy hills and craggy outcroppings; not a great deal else.

"Sir, I am going to give you three seconds..."

Damien rolled his eyes, grunted. "Fine! But this is getting stupid." He tugged the hood back over his head and cursed beneath it.

Why the hell did I agree to this? I feel like a right dickhead.

The bus continued its journey for another five minutes before slowing down and stopping. The passengers sat in silence while they waited to be addressed.

"Can everybody please shuffle to the front of the bus," said a voice that Damien recognised as belonging to the burly man in the black overalls.

Damien got to his feet and felt his way down the aisle. He bumped into someone in front of him and had to wait for them to get moving. Once they did, he followed after them.

At the front of the bus, someone placed a hand on Damien's shoulder and manoeuvred him down the steps. His feet planted down on wet, *crunching* gravel. Someone shoved him from behind and sent him stumbling forward. It wasn't long before he was standing shoulder to shoulder with the rest of his unknown companions as they were corralled into a group.

"Okay, everybody. You can now take off your hoods."

Damien ripped his off and let it fall to the floor. He couldn't help himself from stomping it into the mud. Everybody else in the crowd seemed equally relieved and there was a collective sigh among them.

The man in the black overalls stood in front of the assembled crowd. Several other men had joined him, all wearing jeans and dark jumpers. The jumpers featured the logo of a great staring eye on the left shoulder. It looked like the type of symbol the Masons would use.

Several yards ahead lay a vast complex that resembled a factory unit in many ways. Barbed wire lined the edges of a ten-foot steel fence that ran around the sides and back of the complex. Giant floodlights lit up the entire area. It reminded Damien of a concentration camp.

"Now," said the man in black overalls. "You are about to enter our specially designed facility. Some of you will spend up to ten days inside. Some of you not so long. In order to remain inside you must obey all rules at all times. Failure to follow rules will result in expulsion from the house. Failure to follow commands will result in expulsion from the house. Failure to participate in tasks will result in expulsion from the house. Cameras will be watching your every move. Do all of you understand?"

The crowd mumbled affirmably.

The man continued. "Each day inside the house will include a group task followed by a vote to eliminate one member of the household. The winner or winners of the group task will be immune from receiving votes for twenty four hours. Each evening will feature an elimination task between the two members of the group who received the most votes. The loser of the elimination task will be expelled from the house. Is that clear?"

The crowd mumbled agreement once more.

"After all contestants bar two are eliminated, the prize money will have been won. Two million pounds split between the final two housemates. Those housemates will then have a choice – they can leave with a million pounds each, or wage it against one another in a final elimination task. The winner of the task will then leave the house with two million pounds in cash, while the loser will receive nothing."

The group got excited and began looking around at one another as if to weigh up their competition.

They look like a bunch of rabid hyenas, Damien thought.

The man in the black overalls clapped his hands together, regaining everybody's attention. "Okay, my friends. Welcome to the house and let the games begin."

1

Damien kept to the back of the group as a pair of stiff-looking men led them through the facility. The line of soon-to-be housemates filed down a claustrophobic hallway before entering a steel-framed doorway on their right. It was like a prison door, thick and heavy.

Inside was a room lined on all sides with wooden benches and aluminium lockers. It looked like something you'd find at a sports stadium. Damien noticed that each berth had a name written across it in crude marker pen.

Marker pen? Not very professional.

Damien located the locker with *DAMIEN BANKS* written across it and took a seat in front of it. The other men and women in the room seemed to take his lead and all searched for their own lockers before sitting down too. The man in the black overalls strode into the centre of the room and seemed to smile at their initiative. Damien was getting a little irritated that the man was yet to introduce himself. Manners were important.

Without manners we're just a few steps above a monkey.

The man in the black overalls continued. "Inside your lockers you will find several items. Among those items is a pair of bracelets and a collar. You must clasp these items onto your person and ensure that they are locked tight and secured. Wearing these items is mandatory and will be required for certain tasks inside the house."

Damien stood and turned around. He opened up his locker and located the bracelets and neck ring inside. They were made of a thin, shiny metal that felt very solid despite its low profile. LEDs blinked from various places, which gave them the appearance of something out of a *Star Trek* movie.

It felt totally wrong to shackle himself but Damien placed the collar around his neck and clipped the ends together. They *clacked* and held tight.

They best know how to get this thing off again. I'm not really a collar and cuffs kind of guy.

Next, Damien secured both of the bracelets around his wrists. They were exactly like the neck ring, only smaller. They nipped at his skin until he twisted them around into a more comfortable position. Something on the inside felt sharp.

"Once you have the items attached to your person. Please place all of your personal belongings inside the locker. This includes all jewellery, watches, mobile telephones, and any other communication devices. Future possession of contraband will result in expulsion from the house. Your luggage has been brought to the facility and examined. All authorised items will be brought inside the habitat area of the facility, where you will be entering shortly."

Damien took the sovereign off his finger and the thick chain from around his neck. He placed them inside the locker. His friend back home, Harry, was always on at him to lose the bling, and this was probably the first time he had actually done so. He felt somehow naked without the jewellery.

"Okay. Through that door is the entrance to the house. Inside the house you will find a living area with a large sofa. You are to wait there until further instructions."

Damien looked over at a door set between the rows of lockers. It was made of steel and seemed very secure.

The group reformed their line and one of the security guards ushered them through the open door into the next room.

A woman in front of Damien glanced back at him. She had bright orange hair and was smiling. "Not sure I like the collar and cuffs. A bit much don't you think?"

Damien smiled grimly back at her. He recognised her voice as being the one who had spoken to him on the bus. She'd obviously changed her tune since then and was also getting sick of the theatrics. "You don't have to tell me," Damien said. "This whole thing is a *bit much*. Can't believe I'm even doing this."

She frowned at him with walnut eyes. "Why did you sign up, then?"

"Why you think? The money."

She laughed. It was a feminine sound. "Guess that's why we're all here. That or being famous?"

Damien rolled his eyes. He couldn't think of anything worse than being a 'celebrity'. "You think people are even going to watch the show?" he asked, having not actually paid it much thought. "I mean, isn't this kind of thing a bit old-hat now?"

"People love reality television."

"I suppose they must."

The queue entered an empty reception room and came to a halt. Two more employees with eye-logo sweatshirts were standing inside; both were large and imposing like granite statues.

There was another door in front of the group and they were asked to enter through it, so they carried on forwards until they found themselves inside a vast living room. It was actually quite homely compared to the industrial feeling of the rest of the complex. A giant green sofa occupied the centre of the room in a horseshoe shape and looked big enough to seat everybody comfortably. An open-sided kitchen area lay behind it with several brand-new, sparkling appliances. Obviously no expense had been spared in setting up the 'habitat'.

A long glass window with a sliding patio door ran the length of the far wall. There must have been a garden outside, but it was too dark and too rainy to see at the moment.

Each corner of the room had a blinking camera set ten feet above the ground.

The door the group had entered through suddenly slammed shut.

Damien turned on his heels. The man in black overalls and his burly colleagues were all gone. The only thing that remained in their place was a heavy metal door.

The housemates were locked in.

The competition had begun.

Am I really doing this? Do I even have a chance of winning?
Christ, I really need that money.

The woman with the bright orange hair came up to Damien and gave him another one of her beaming smiles. "I'm Jules. Good to meet you....?"

Damien shook her hand and nodded. "Damien."

"Damien? Like that evil little boy in the movies?"

Damien rolled his eyes. "Yeah, if you like."

"So, Damien, what should we do?"

He shrugged. "They said to wait here. Maybe we should all just take a seat. I'm dead on my feet anyway."

Jules nodded and rubbed at her eyes, smudging her eyeliner a little. "Me too. I thought we were never going to get here. Now that we have, though, I'm so excited."

"You don't even know what to expect."

"That's why I'm excited. Don't you just love the unknown?"

"No, you can't prepare for the unknown."

"Sometimes it's nice not to be in control."

"I'll take your word for it."

Everybody in the room began to mingle. Damien did a quick head count. He found that there were six women and five other men. Twelve people in total, including him.

Eleven people between me and millions of pounds.

He took a seat on the long sofa with Jules and they continued their conversation. A guy with slicked-back blonde hair and a finely-tailored suit took it upon himself to come join them.

"Hey," he said. "My name is Alex. I work in banking. How about you two?"

"I'm a carpenter," Damien replied, wondering what a banker was doing there. It couldn't be for the money with all that they earned.

"I'm unemployed," said Jules. "I used to run a salon with my sister but she killed herself and...well, things kind of just fell apart after that. This competition is my chance to get back on my feet, you know? Even if I don't win, I might get a gig on television or something like that. I just want to move on, and this seemed like a good way."

"A bit drastic, maybe," said Damien. "But I guess that makes sense."

"So, what will you do with the money if you win?" Alex asked him, running a hand through his greased blonde hair. "I want to set up a real estate business in Dubai, but I need more capital. I have half-a-mil already, but winning this thing will really make sure that my business is a success."

Damien didn't reply. The pursuit of fortune wasn't something that interested him very much. If you spent your whole life trying to get rich, you only ended up wasting life in the process. Life was for living, not accumulating wealth that you could never hope to spend.

Seeing as how I am currently prostituting myself to win a million, I guess that makes me a hypocrite. My reasons for needing the money are less selfish.

Damien realised that both Jules and Alex were staring at him, waiting for a response.

"Well?" Jules said. "What do you want to do with the money, Damien?"

He shrugged his shoulders and looked away, examining the other housemates that were mingling with one another like dogs at a park. "My reason for wanting the money is personal....*private*. All I'll say is that I need it."

"Amen to that," said Alex. "Two million quid can fulfil a lot of *needs*."

"It's only one million," said Jules. "Unless you're willing to bet it all at the end against whoever is left."

"Got to go for the kill," said Alex, clicking his fingers on each hand sharply like a pair of firing guns. "No point getting to the end of this thing only to split the winnings."

Jules wiggled her eyebrows at him playfully. "So, you'll definitely go head to head if you get to the end?"

"Absolutely."

Jules turned her focus back to Damien. "How about you? Will you bet one million to turn it into two?"

Damien shrugged his shoulders. "I only need one. I'm happy to share."

Jules seemed to think about things for a moment, chewed on her bottom lip. "I'm happy to share, too," she eventually said. "One million is more than enough. Lots more than I have now. Besides, if I get to the end of the show, I'm sure I'll make more money from TV deals and stuff."

"I hadn't even thought about that," said Alex, clicking his fingers again. "I could be set up for life. I could buy a hundred properties in Dubai." He smiled greedily.

Damien wondered how the banker would react if he got eliminated from the competition early on. It seemed as if the peroxide-headed man had no contemplation of not winning. It was a foregone conclusion in his mind.

Good luck to him. Nothing wrong with having confidence...

Whether it's warranted or not.

There was a static hiss followed by an ear-piercing whine. A booming voice filled the living area and seemed to be coming from a hidden speaker so loud that it would have held itself proud at a German rave.

"WELCOME HOUSEMATES. I AM THE LANDLORD. YOU WILL OBEY ME AT ALL TIMES. FAILURE TO DO SO WILL RESULT IN PAIN. TRYING TO ESCAPE WILL RESULT IN PAIN. MISBEHAVIOUR OF ANY KIND WILL RESULT IN PAIN."

The housemates looked at one another with confusion. As much as they understood that they were taking part in a game, the voice from the speakers was unnervingly authoritative, and the words were unsettling to say the least.

"What do you think he means by 'pain'?" Jules asked.

Damien shook his head and frowned. "I don't know."

"IN A FEW MOMENTS YOU WILL BE PRESENTED WITH A VIEWING SCREEN. YOU WILL PAY ATTENTION TO THIS SCREEN AT ALL TIMES. IF AN INSTRUCTION APPEARS ON THE SCREEN, YOU WILL FOLLOW IT."

One of the walls, the one opposite the long glass window and patio door, began to open up. A pair of secret panels slid apart to reveal an alcove within. The alcove held a television screen that must have been at least sixty-inches wide.

"THE VIEWING SCREEN HAS A 4K RESOLUTION. IT IS CUTTING EDGE TECHNOLOGY. EVERYTHING INSIDE THIS HOUSE IS CUTTING EDGE TECHNOLOGY. YOU ARE FREE TO ENJOY ALL FACILITIES WHEN NOT UNDERTAKING A TASK OR INSTRUCTION. USE THE NEXT TWELVE HOURS TO REST AND RECUPERATE. YOU WILL NEED YOUR ENERGY. WE WILL BEGIN TOMORROW."

The speaker whined and crackled, and then went silent. The television screen illuminated brightly and then went dark. It remained blank except for a single word displayed boldly across its centre: RELAX.

2

Damien made an effort to get to know the other housemates during the last hour or so. He wasn't the most sociable person, but he would fare much better over the following days if he tried to integrate himself as much as possible. Just as he had dreaded, however, the other housemates were a predicable mixture of wannabe celebrities and those who just wanted to get rich quick. They were vain and inwardly focused – possibly even sociopathic in some cases. Damien understood their personalities. They were a product of society, a society obsessed with surface rather than depth. He had once lived a similar existence himself. If it were not for his friend, Harry, he would have been no different to the other house-mates, chasing money, sex, and worthless adoration from strangers.

Among the colourful group was a chain-smoking exotic dancer, covered in tattoos, named Jade; a retired school teacher, with a shock of white hair, called Patrick; and a stubble-faced mechanic called Richard. The man was pretty uncouth and seemed to swear almost every other word.

There were also many other personalities inside the house, but Damien had yet to memorise their names or scope them out thoroughly.

"What say we check this place out?" suggested the exotic dancer, Jade, a cigarette clutched between two talon-like fingernails. When she spoke, she spoke loud, as if she thought merely doing so would be enough to make her important. In this instance everybody seemed to be happy to follow her lead. Damien was also interested in exploring the place that would be his home for the next ten days, so he stood up and followed after Jade. She was heading for a door near the kitchen. The word PANTRY was written across it. Jade grabbed a hold of the handle and gave it a hefty yank.

Her face lit up when she saw what was behind the door.

"Oh hell yes! We're in for some shits and giggles tonight, peeps."

Damien wasn't as impressed by what he saw. In fact it made him groan. The pantry was stacked full of beer and wine and cigarettes. There were also snacks and soft drinks, but it was clear that the show producers wanted alcohol to play a large part of the group's activities inside the house. Damien had expected it would be the case, having seen similar reality shows, but having it confirmed kind of sucked. Damien didn't drink.

He glanced up at the nearest camera.

Now we're all but guaranteed to have fireworks and they're just waiting to film it.

Everybody whooped at the sight of so much party fuel and started handing it out.

Over in the kitchen, the blond guy, Alex, was rooting through cupboards and opening up drawers. "There's a shit-load of food here," he suddenly yelled out, clicking his fingers to an imaginary rhythm that must have been playing in his head. "And we have steaks and some big fat sausages in the freezer."

"Splendid," said Patrick, licking his lips. "I love a bit of fresh meat."

"There's a toilet over here," someone shouted. "No bathroom, though. Weird."

Jade took a bottle of red wine out of the fridge and palmed off the screw top. She sauntered into the living area and took a swig directly from the bottle. Damien winced.

Classy bird.

"So," Jade said, taking another swig and wiping away the wine that found its way onto her bony chin. "Let's see what's through door number two."

She approached another door that was at the far corner of the living area. It, too, had a label affixed across its top, but it was too far away for Damien to read. He took a few steps closer until he could see what it said.

ELIMINATION CHAMBER.

"Must be where we do the tasks," Jade guessed. "I can't wait."

"That just leaves the bedrooms," said the stubble-faced mechanic, Richard. "So where the fuck are they?"

Damien looked around. There were no more doors.

"They have to be somewhere," said Jade. "Everybody take a look around."

The housemates dispersed, searching for a door that they might have missed. After several minutes of investigation, though, everybody came up short.

"There aren't any more doors," said Jules, tucking her bright orange hair behind her ears. The makeup around her eyes was still smudged which made it look like she had been crying.

"There has to be," said Alex.

"Then where?"

Alex marched up to the long garden windows and tried the patio door. "Locked," he said, rattling the handle. He adjusted his tie and cricked his neck. "They must be playing games with us."

Jade let out a feline growl and folded her brightly coloured arms. "Okay, very amusing. Can someone please tell us where our beds are, please!" She strode into the centre of the living area and stared up at the ceiling as if addressing some deity in the clouds. "Excuse me....Mr Landlord, or whatever you're called. Can you tell us where we're sleeping tonight, thank you very much?"

There was no reply. The house's concealed speakers remained silent.

"HEY, YOU RETARD. STOP SCREWING AROUND AND TELL US WHERE OUR BEDS ARE!" Jade threw the bottle of wine in her hand across the room, smashing it against the nearest wall and leaving a deep red stain that was not unlike blood.

Damien raised an eyebrow in surprise. *Wow! She's like a spoiled kid.*

Richard was covering his mouth with his hand, disguising a laugh as he watched the commotion. To him it was obviously some form of entertainment to watch another person lose it.

Jade glanced around in obvious frustration. It was clear that she was going to blow some kind of mental fuse at any moment. The girl was unstable, that much quickly became clear.

Damien stepped forward, put a hand up to calm her. "They're just messing with us, Jade. This is all for television, right? Well, looks like the games have begun already. Don't let them get to you, okay?"

"Yeah," Alex agreed. "If you go off like a firework you're liable to get yourself thrown out. And that means no prize money for you!" He actually seemed quite pleased by the notion.

Jade was breathing heavily. She glanced around for a few moments like a nervous chicken. Eventually the rise and fall of her heaving chest started to shorten and a semblance of calm returned to her harsh, angular features. It was like a switch had been flipped, sending her someplace else for a while, but now she was returning to reality.

"You're right," she said. "You're right. They want me to blow my lid so they can get some juicy footage for the cameras." She looked over at one of the cameras and extended her middle finger. "Well, you're not going to get one over on me so easily. Swivel on this."

Damien shook his head and sighed. *Great, I'm stuck inside this house with a bloody loon. I hope they allowed her to keep her medication*

"Well," Jules interjected. "I say that we just forget about our sleeping arrangements for now and get our S-W-A-G on instead! Let's party."

Damien rolled his eyes. *Great! Someone just used the word 'party' as a verb.*

I'm screwed.

Jade grinned, large and wide. Her frustration seemed completely gone now. She hurried back over to the pantry and grabbed two more bottles of wine, holding them aloft her head like trophies. "Who's got the glasses?"

Alex clicked his fingers like guns. "Let me help you, sweetheart."

3

Without his watch on, Damien had no idea what time it was. He assumed it was early morning and that the sun would make an appearance any minute. The rain still poured, but seemed to be letting up slightly. Its earlier *rat-a-tat-tat* on the window pane had given way to a gentle *pitter patter*.

The other housemates had drunk their fair share of alcohol by now. Damien had stuck to soft drinks and water, much to the chagrin of the others. They had treated him like he was ill somehow – like sobriety was some new form of leprosy. Tracey, a slender woman in a blouse and smart grey trousers had tried on several occasions throughout the night to get him to drink. She had become quite pissy when he refused for the third or fourth time.

As he watched them, though, falling around and chatting utter nonsense to one another, he was glad for his abstinence. People did not realise the power of alcohol and how much of their dignity it could soak through. It was worse than drugs, in Damien's opinion.

The stuff almost killed Harry once upon a time.

Still, if there was anything positive to dwell on at all, it was that at least the housemates had a decent sense of humour. There had been many a joke or humorous quip made in the last several hours and even Damien had cracked a smile now and then. It was only in the last thirty minutes or so that things had devolved into drunken nonsense. People's eyeballs had begun to roll around like loose marbles in their skulls and their speech had turned to incoherent slurry. Damien was now acutely aware of being the only sober person in the room. *A rabbit among foxes.* He wanted very much now to find a bed and get some sleep. The metal ring around his neck had started to feel heavy. The ones around his wrists were starting to chafe.

"You're not like the others," said a woman with Mediterranean features and a slender, petite frame. She had introduced herself to him earlier and said that her name was 'Danni'. She had streaky brown hair and wore a crisp white blouse above a short black skirt. Her legs were long, sleek and tanned. They had caught Damien's lustful stare on more than one occasion throughout the night and he hoped his leching had not been caught by the cameras. He tried to be a better man than that.

But I'm still only human.

He frowned at the woman as she took the seat beside him. "What do you mean, 'I'm not like the others'?"

She smirked at him as if he were being deliberately ignorant. "I mean that you're not in here to get famous. You're not fanning your feathers like a peacock and trying to get attention like everybody else. I don't think the thought of being a celebrity appeals to you at all."

"It doesn't."

"Then my question is: why did you apply to be on a reality TV show if you have no interest in fame?"

Damien cleared his throat and looked away. "I'm just trying to repay a favour. I need the prize money."

Danni crossed her slender legs and leant in closer to him. He could smell the alcohol on her breath and it tempted him to grab a beer for himself. The hoppy odour took him back to his wilder days where he would have been the life of the party, instead of just a spectator. But, as much as he missed the feeling of inebriation, he was adamant never to go back there.

Danni was pulling a face at him. "You want to repay a favour?"

He nodded. "Yeah, and that's all I want to say about it."

Danni wasn't put off by his hostile tone. She nodded thoughtfully and looked him in the eye. "Fair enough. My reasons for being here are my own as well. I'm not like the others either. Being famous is the last thing I want."

"And yet you are here like me."

"Yes, I am. Maybe we have similar agendas. Maybe we should form a pact."

Damien huffed. "I think I'll be okay by myself."

She raised an eyebrow, thin and curvy. "You think so? The other housemates are here to party and cause chaos. When they see you sitting here and judging them like you've been doing all night, they're going to vote for you every time. If you want that prize money. You have to start thinking smart."

Damien thought about it. As much as he hated being inside the house, he was there for a reason. If he didn't win at least some of the money then this whole thing was a colossal waste of time. And he would have failed a dear friend.

"Okay," he said. "I'll think about it. Let's just see what tomorrow brings first."

DANNI SMILED and rubbed a hand on his thigh. "I'm looking forward to it."

Damien sighed. "I'm not."

DAY 2

Damien's back was aching when he opened his eyes. The sun was out and shining through the long glass window. But it was a dull sunlight and looked in no way warm.

Damien was sprawled back on the sofa with his legs stretched out on the floor. It took him a moment to get his blurry mind focused and figure out what was going on. The smell of stale cigarette smoke and standing alcohol brought it all rushing back.

Must have fallen asleep. Wonder what time it is.

Oh yeah, that's right. No watch.

Some of the other housemates were already milling about, nursing obvious hangovers with tall glasses of water, while the rest slept on the sofa alongside Damien. Danni was still beside him, snoring softly with her head tilted back on the cushion. The metal collar around her neck blinked green from its LED lights. She still managed to look pretty somehow. Her long legs still managed to catch his gaze.

Alex came over to the sofa and handed Damien a glass of water. The man's eyes were red and bleary, his cheeks blotchy. His tie was loose and his top button was undone, while his slicked-back blond hair was hanging limply across his forehead.

Damien took the drink and thanked him.

"Think we'd have been better off following your lead," he said. "I feel like a bag of shit. Tracey's been throwing up in the toilet for over an hour. God knows what percent that wine was."

"When did you wake up?" Damien asked him.

"Wake up? Most of us haven't been to bed yet. Not that we've actually been given any beds to sleep in. You got a couple hours, though. I envy you."

"Did I? Feels like I was out longer." Damien pointed his toes and sighed as his calf muscles shuddered awake. He got to his feet and rolled his shoulders, cracked his neck. "Right, well, I could do with something to eat. I'll go see what I can rustle up."

Alex clicked his fingers and pointed them at Damien like guns. "Good man. You'll be the most popular guy in the room if you can find some bacon."

"I'll see what I can do."

A large, barrel-chested bald man stood in the kitchen, pouring a pint of milk with a meaty hand covered in scars. He looked up with a fag in his mouth at Damien and nodded. "How's it going?" He managed to speak while still holding the cigarette in his mouth.

Damien nodded back at him. "Good, thanks. Sorry, I can't quite remember your name."

"Chris. Don't forget it again."

Damien smiled, but wasn't entirely sure if the guy was being serious. The dirty black stubble and wide scar across the larger man's chin gave him a menacing look that suggested any sense of humour was completely absent.

"I'm Damien, by the way. I was going to see if I can rustle us up some breakfast."

"Want me to go get you an apron and some tampons?"

Damien frowned and cleared his throat. "I'm sorry, what?"

"Let the split arses do the cooking. You're not a split arse, are you?"

Damien shook his head and sighed. "Seriously, dude. It's not the fifties anymore. Besides, I like to cook."

The bigger guy just pulled his face into a frown and walked away, shaking his head and chuckling to himself. Apparently Damien's intention to cook was highly amusing to Chris.

Don't see him making many fans amongst the ladies of the house.

Either that or they'll be falling all over him. You never can tell with women.

I certainly got more interest back when I was an arsehole. That was definitely one of the fringe benefits.

Damien headed over to the kitchen's large refrigerator and yanked the door open. To his delight there was a shelf piled high with bacon rashers. The door's inside compartment housed a dozen eggs.

If I can find some bread, we're all set.

Damien turned around to check the cupboards for the rest of what he needed and was greeted by Danni. Her brown eyes were sleepy but a pleasant smile adorned her face.

"Hey, partner. Want some help?"

"I haven't said I'm your partner, but sure. I would love some help. We need bread."

Danni went over to a cupboard and pulled out a loaf of

half-white. "Spotted it last night," she said. "What are we making?"

"Bacon and egg sandwiches."

"I think Jade is a vegetarian."

"Then she can feed herself."

Danni laughed. "You're not really a morning person, are you?"

"Not really an anytime person. This is all a bit bizarre to me, being around so many strangers."

Danni stepped behind him and started rubbing at his trapezius muscles. "We won't all be strangers for long," she said. "After a day or two we'll all be settled in. Besides, people will be getting voted out every day, so it won't be long before the numbers start to thin out."

Damien nodded. He liked the sound of that. The house would already benefit from seeing the back of thugs like Chris and temperamental divas like Jade. As much as he found Danni presumptive – and invasive with the way she was massaging his shoulders – she was probably the most tolerable person in the house.

"So did you get much sleep?" he asked her, moving out of the grasp of her kneading palms and turning around to face her.

She moved to the counter and started pulling slices of bread out of the bag. She placed them down in a line. "I got a little bit. I must have zonked out right after you did."

Damien rooted around a low cupboard and found some frying pans. He placed them on top of the kitchen's range cooker and lit the gas hob. "I was completely knackered after all that travelling," he said.

"Me, too. They drove me all the way up from Kent. I was stuck in a car for twelve hours."

Damien winced. "Wow, I thought *I* had it bad. Strange

that they didn't just fly you up. I mean, it's not very TV-like to stick one of their stars in a cramped saloon for that long. A flight to Edinburgh would have been – what? – a couple hundred quid?"

Danni stopped what she was doing and looked at him. "Hmm," she said. "I guess it wouldn't have cost very much. I suppose they're just trying to stress us all out, make us tired and more prone to combustion. You know how much reality TV producers love a bit of tension."

Damien nodded. "Unfortunately that's what people seem to enjoy watching."

"Human nature. We love conflict."

"Not all of us do."

"You think us all philistines, don't you, Damien?"

Damien grabbed a couple of eggs and began cracking them into one of the pans which he had just laced with cooking oil. "I don't think I'm better than anybody else, but I have a better grasp on my priorities than most."

"How old are you?"

He shrugged. "Twenty-three, why?"

Danni patted him on the rump with an unexpected slap. "Because you're twenty-three-going-on-fifty. Try to remember that you're still young."

Damien broke another egg. He knew he was prone to being a stick-in-the-mud, but it was just the way he was – at least how he was lately.

"I'll try to loosen up," he said. "No promises, though."

4

The egg and bacon sandwiches went down well. Everybody, with the exception of Jade who had located some cereal for herself, polished them off in minutes. It was perfect timing because, right when they were finishing off the last morsels, the voice of The Landlord came over the speakers.

"IN EXACTLY TWO MINUTES, THE DOOR TO THE GARDEN WILL OPEN."

That was it. The speaker crackled and went dead.

"The plot thickens," said Danni.

"I hope they have a hot tub," said Jules, sweeping back her orange hair so that it sat behind her ears.

"They always do on these things," said Alex. "They want to see us all naked."

"Let me have a few more drinks," said Jade, "And they might get to."

Two minutes went by and the patio door clicked.

Jade was the first one there, shoving people aside on her quest to be at the front of the pack. She pulled down the handle and slid the patio door aside. The cold, autumn air came whistling in from outside, along with some sideways-falling rain.

"Wow," said Jules. "I had no idea the weather was so shit from in here."

Damien agreed with her. The glass windows must have been double – or maybe even triple – glazed.

"Well, I hope they're going to give us our luggage," said an older woman named Catherine, "because it's not right letting us freeze out in the cold. My creaking bones can't take it."

"I totally forgot about our luggage," Jules said, folding her arms to fight off the chill.

Everybody filed out into the garden and started looking around. To Jade's glee there was indeed a hot tub bubbling away and emitting the recognisable smell of chlorine. There were also a couple of benches around the perimeter and a long picnic table at one corner. The whole area was laid out like a grassy central courtyard, with buildings on all four sides. Directly opposite was an open door, but the other two buildings, the ones to the left and right of the courtyard, were just brick walls; no doors or even any windows. What one of the walls did have was a huge painting of the staring eye that seemed to be the television show's logo. A large CCTV camera sat immediately above it.

"That door over there is open," said Jules, pointing.

"Yeah it is," Damien concurred. "Let's go check it out."

Luckily Jade was already stripping down to her undies and leaping into the hot tub. It meant he could check out the other building in peace.

The grassy area in the centre of the courtyard was almost a perfect square of about sixty-feet. It was large and heavily waterlogged, which meant it took them a good few paces before they reached the building on the opposite side.

The door still remained open, just slightly ajar, suggesting it was okay to enter.

Damien pushed the door wider and stepped through. He was pleased by what he found, but also a little dismayed.

Guess this is the bedroom.

Not exactly five-star.

The large room consisted of six single beds – not enough to supply them all with a place to sleep. It could, of course, be just one of two bedrooms, one for the men and one for the girls. What really worried Damien, though, was the state of the beds themselves. They were antiques. Grimy sheets covered the threadbare mattresses atop rickety metal frames. They were not even fit to bed prisoners in.

"No way am I sleeping on one of those," said Danni, who entered the room behind them.

"Me either," said Jules. "What the fu-"

"It's just another game," said Damien. "To see how we react."

Jules sighed and prodded at the bracelets on her skinny wrists. They looked like giant bangles in the dim light. "So you think there's a real bedroom hidden somewhere?"

Damien shrugged his shoulders. He was regretting his decision to enter the house more and more. "Maybe," he said. "Or perhaps this is it."

"It can't be!"

"Makes sense," said Danni. "With only six beds, there's going to be conflict between us, choosing who gets one and who doesn't. The mere fact that the beds are so awful is going to lead to a lot of grouchiness."

Jules leant back against the nearest wall and seemed to deflate. "They must really want us to kill each other."

"I wouldn't go that far," said Damien, "but it sure looks like they're hoping for some good television."

"What the hell, man?" It was Alex. He had entered the bedroom and was now staring around in disbelief. His sleeves were rolled up to the elbows and his smart suit jacket was gone. He looked a little sweaty and pale. "This can't be the bedroom. There's not even enough places to sleep."

"All part of the fun, I suppose," said Damien. "I don't want to sleep in one those things, anyway. I'm happy to opt out of having one."

"Me too," said Danni.

"Suit yourselves," Jules said and headed off to the row of beds, "but even this is better than no bed at all."

"They're all dirty," said Danni, wrinkling her dark eyebrows and screwing up her plump lips in distaste.

Jules stared back at the other woman as if she were an idiot. "It's just theatrics. They probably just stained it with stage paint or something. It's not going to be real muck on the sheets."

"Well, I'm not taking the chance," said Danni. "You're welcome to it."

"What about you, Alex?" Jules asked. "Best claim one now or you may not be able to later."

Alex looked at Damien and Danni for a few seconds and then shrugged his shoulders. "Better than the floor," he said, and then took the bed next to the one that Jules had picked out for herself.

Danni leant into Damien and placed a hand on his back. "See," she said. "Alliances are already forming."

Damien looked at her and let out a sigh. He had no doubt that alliances would begin to form, but that didn't mean that one was needed to win.

He walked away from Danni and re-entered the garden.

If I win this thing, I plan on doing it with my integrity intact.

No alliances, no tactics. I'm just going to be me and hope that's good enough.

Harry wouldn't accept it any other way.

Suddenly Damien started to feel like winning the money might be out of his reach.

5

Whatever everybody else saw the state of their sleeping arrangements they had been angry, yet had slowly come to the same conclusion: it was all part of the game. It was decided that the beds would be divvied up later and that those without would make do on the large sofa in the living area. It was only a problem if they made it one.

The garden was chilly, but it was where half the group had congregated since the rain had stopped. Jade and a handful of others had settled into the hot tub with a bottle of wine and a pack of cigarettes, while the other housemates took naps in various places both inside and out.

Damien was sitting alone at the picnic table, his hands clutched together in front of him. There was a stain on its wooden surface that looked a little like paint or maybe even blood. It wouldn't be the first time a clumsy woodman had left a piece of himself on the furniture he made.

Damien was thinking about Harry and feeling guilty for having left him alone to run the business for the next two weeks. They worked well together. They were a team.

Leaving behind their small woodwork shop felt like a neglect of duties. But Harry was the reason he was doing this. Harry needed money and Damien was trying to get it for him. He just hoped that his friend understood.

Course he does. Harry is the most compassionate person I know.

At least he was until recently...

I really shouldn't have left him alone.

Damien's mind was just about to take him down a dark alleyway when two people sat on the bench opposite.

The couple were Lewis and Sarah. Lewis was an immigrant from the Ivory Coast, but had come to the UK as a child and, as such, had a strong Manchester accent. Sarah was an Office Supply Manager from Luton. The inactivity of her job was present on her curvy hips.

Damien nodded to them both but chose not to speak. Sometimes he felt it easier to read people if you let them do the talking.

Lewis was the one to start. "How you doing, mate? Bit surreal being in here, innit?"

Damien nodded.

"You doing okay?"

Damien nodded again.

"You're Damien, right?"

Damien nodded.

"Sorry, are we annoying you?" said Sarah.

Damien shook his head.

"It's just that you're not talking back to us."

Damien thought about his intention to integrate and decided to open up before he annoyed them too much. "I was just a bit lost in thought. Sorry."

"That's alright, mate," said Lewis. "I get lost in a

daydream now and then as well. So, what were you doing before you signed up to the show?"

"Just working, I guess."

"And what do you do, Damien?" Sarah asked. She seemed to be getting a little irritated by his reticence.

"I'm a carpenter," he said, forcing a polite smile. "I run a little woodwork factory with my business partner. We sell bespoke pieces mainly, but we also help out local charities with various things they need. We just recently outfitted the local church with new pews."

Sarah's eyes went wide. "Wow! I wouldn't have expected that from seeing you. No offence, but you don't seem like the caring type."

"Really?" said Damien. "How so?"

"You just come across as a bit...*standoffish.*"

"I'm just not good with people," he admitted. "Perhaps I was hoping to overcome that by coming here." It was a lie, of course, but he hoped it sounded convincing.

"Well, I'm sure you'll have no problem making friends if you win a million quid," said Lewis with a greedy sparkle in his round eyes.

"Or two," Sarah added, giggling and covering her mouth with a pudgy hand.

Damien nodded his head. "Definitely. Is the money the main reason that you're both here?"

The two of them nodded. Lewis said, "Don't think I can take the rat race much longer, mate. I dream of spending my days on a beach in Saint Lucia."

"Hey, that sounds nice," said Sarah, turning to him and grinning. "Maybe I'll come with you."

"Make it three," said Damien giving another insincere smile.

"ALL HOUSEMATES, PLEASE GATHER IN THE GARDEN."

It was voice of The Landlord. Damien frowned. He didn't feel like getting up.

Got to play by the rules, though.

Those who were inside the house filed outside quickly. Jade and the others in the hot tub quickly towelled themselves off and pulled their clothes back on.

Once everybody was gathered together in the centre of the grassy courtyard the landlord spoke again.

"IN ONE MINUTE. YOU WILL BE PRESENTED WITH TWO CONTAINERS. EACH CONTAINER IS FULL OF HOUEMATES LUGGAGE."

"Sweet," said Jules. "I want to grab a jumper. My nips are turning to rubber."

Everybody waited, looking around and wondering where exactly these containers were going to appear. Then the ground began to move, right in front of the huge painting of the eye logo.

At the leftmost edge of the courtyard, a wide platform began to rise up on hydraulic stilts. The platform was topped with grass and had been indistinguishable from the rest of the ground until it had started to rise up on metal cylinders.

"That's pretty trippy," said Lewis. "I would never have even known it was there."

Beneath the grassy platform was a pair of windowed enclosures. They looked a bit like space-age transporter pods from a sci-fi show. Each of the two glass pods was filled with suitcases.

"That's our luggage," Jade shouted excitedly. "Thank fudge for that. I need my makeup. I look like a panda."

The platform stopped moving and locked audibly into place. Everyone in the garden looked around in confusion.

"Do we try and open them?" Alex asked. He was back in his suit jacket again and had readjusted his tie.

"BEHIND THESE TWO CONTAINERS IS A PAIR OF HANDHELD PUMPS. THESE PUMPS ARE ATTACHED TO A PAIR OF HOSES. TWO HOUSEMATES MUST BRING EACH HOSE INTO THE CENTRE OF THE GARDEN."

Everyone looked around at one another. Jade stepped forward and a half-second later, so did Alex. The two of them trod gingerly towards the glass containers and then navigated around to the back of them. They reappeared moments later with steel pipes the length of broom handles. The pipes were both attached to long red hoses.

The apparatus seemed heavy and both Alex and Jade seemed to struggle while dragging them along the grass towards the rest of the group. When they finally managed it, The Landlord gave further instructions.

"JADE AND ALEX. YOU HAVE OFFERED YOURSELF UP AS LEADERS. CHOOSE YOUR TEAMS AND MAKE THEM EQUAL."

Jade shrugged at Alex. "I'll pick then you pick, one at a time, yeah?"

Alex shrugged.

"I pick Tracey," said Jade.

Tracey sauntered over to her teammate and smiled. Then she stood with a hand on her slender hip as if she were giving a pose to the paparazzi.

Maybe she's playing up for the cameras.

"I pick Damien," said Alex.

Surprised to be picked so soon, Damien headed over to Alex and nodded his thanks.

Jade made her next pick. "Catherine." Catherine was another person that Damien was yet to really make an acquaintance with. She was the oldest housemate, along with the retired school teacher, Patrick. She wore thick round glasses which, along with her shrivelled face, made her look a little like a mole.

Alex picked Jules.

Jade picked the big guy, Chris.

Alex: "Danni."

Jade: "Lewis."

"Patrick."

"Sarah."

Alex made the final pick. "Richard."

"NOW THAT YOU HAVE PICKED YOUR TEAMS, THE GAME CAN BEGIN. IN YOUR GROUPS, YOU EACH POSSESS A PUMP – NOT UNLIKE A BICYCLE PUMP. YOU MUST GRAB THE HANDLE AS A TEAM AND PUMP AIR INTO YOUR HOSES. THESE HOSES ARE CONNECTED TO A HYDRAULIC WATER TANK. THE FIRST TEAM TO FILL THEIR GLASS CONTAINER WITH LIQUID WILL WIN THE TASK."

Damien cleared his throat. "I don't get it," he said. "If we fill the tanks up with liquid the luggage inside will be ruined."

"THE TASK WILL BEGIN IN 10...9...8..."

"Hey," said Damien. "This doesn't make any sense."

"7...6...5..."

"Just get ready," Alex ordered. "We need to win this."

"4...3...2..."

Damien was about to protest further but decided there was no point. Being in the house meant submitting his will to the producers. If they wanted to mess around with him, what choice did he have? It was what he had signed up for and he would just have to go along for the ride.

"I... START PUMPING."

Both teams began pumping frantically. Damien was a second or two late in helping his team due to his initial confusion. It was hard work to hold the pump firmly. The hose thrashed about wildly. Damien grabbed the lower portion of the pump and held it tightly so that the others could work the handle more steadily.

The glass containers at the back of the courtyard began to rain liquid from their ceilings. They almost looked like the gunge booths you saw on Saturday morning kid's shows."

"Come on," shouted Alex, sweat already forming on his brow. His Adam's apple bobbed beneath his collar. "Their tank is filling faster. Pump!"

Damien struggled to hold the pump steady while his teammates worked away on the handle. Every successful pump resulted in a hiss of air entering the hose and a gush of liquid entering the tank. The containers were filling quickly. The liquid inside was clear except for the slightly brown hue that seemed to swirl in random currents.

Both teams pumped furiously, all of them growing tired. Their faces bloomed red and their movements became slower and jerkier as if moving through clay.

As the tanks became almost full, the contest was more or less even. Alex's team were just a pump or two behind Jade's.

"Come on, come on," said Alex. "We're almost there."

A siren went off.

"We did it," cried Jade. "We won!"

Alex looked over at the other team's tank. It was full to the brim with the mysterious liquid. He threw the pump down on the floor and hissed. "Sod it!"

"Sorry," said Damien. "We'll win the next one."

Alex shook his head and scowled. "If you hadn't been messing around at the beginning we would have won."

Damien felt a twinge of aggression in his gut, a tiger being poked. He took a deep breath and petted it into submission. "Like I said, I'm sorry."

"Don't worry about it," said Danni. "It's just a game."

"A game we just kicked your arses at," said Jade from over in her group. She was dancing around barefoot like an excited child.

Alex muttered something under his breath. Damien tried to reach out to the guy and apologise again, but was shrugged away for his efforts.

"Get the hell off me."

Damien tried to look apologetic, but he was finding it difficult to ignore the guy's bad attitude. "Just chill, Alex. It doesn't matter."

"Don't tell me to chill. You just lost us this task."

"And you might lose the next one, so cut me some slack and I'll do the same for you in the future."

"HOUSEMATES, THE TASK IS COMPLETE. JADE'S TEAM HAS FILLED THEIR CONTAINER."

Suddenly the liquid inside Jade's team's container ignited. The fluid inside must have been petrol or some other combustible liquid. The flames swirled around inside the obviously tempered glass. Smoke escaped from the top of the platform via an unseen vent.

"What the hell?" said Jade. "That's our luggage in there. They're burning our luggage."

Damien stared into the flames as they continued to rage and consume. Leather and plastic melted and popped.

The other container, the one that had belonged to Alex's team, began to drain away. The liquid disappeared through the bottom of the glass compartment until it was once again empty of everything except for the luggage inside.

Then it popped open like an Easter egg.

"JADE'S TEAM. YOU MAY COLLECT THE LUGGAGE FROM THE LOSER'S CONTAINER. THIS LUGGAGE IS YOURS TO KEEP, REGARDLESS OF ITS FORMER OWNER."

Alex and the rest of his team looked at one another with confusion and a certain degree of persecution. Damien was perplexed. What exactly did The Landlord mean that Jade's team could 'keep the luggage regardless of its former owner'?

Jade and her team wasted no time. They hurried up to the open container and began dragging out the cases inside. Six pieces of luggage in total – all random. They were sealed in plastic bags which had protected them from the liquid. Damien spotted his own suitcase immediately.

"Hey, that one is mine," said Damien, pointing to the black shell case.

It was in the hands of Chris, who looked at him with an unfriendly sneer. "You lost, mate."

"Don't be unreasonable. My things are in there."

Chris smirked. The expression made the thick scar on his chin stretch wider. "*My* things."

Damien took a step forward but Danni stopped him. "He's just playing by their rules," she said. "Let him. With a million pounds you can buy a whole lot more stuff."

Damien didn't like it, someone else taking his belongings. He wasn't the type of person to take shit from bullies like Chris. He was the type of guy to stand up to them. But he also had a temper, a temper he couldn't always control.

I don't get involved with confrontation anymore. I just need to stay calm and let it go. Be the bigger man.

"Oh yes!" cried Jade, struggling with a large purple suitcase. "I got my own things."

"Me too," said Lewis and Catherine.

It appeared, however, that Tracey and Sarah had the luggage of somebody else. The fact was given away by the disappointed frowns on their faces.

"Who do these belong to?" Sarah asked.

Jules and Patrick put their hands up.

"Then you might as well take them. I wouldn't feel right wearing somebody else's clothes. Besides, one of these will be full of men's clothes."

"I suppose that I agree," said Tracey, shrugging her shoulders. The two ladies handed over the luggage to their rightful owners. That left everybody looking at Chris who was still in possession of Damien's suitcase.

"What you lookin' at?" he grunted at them.

"Well," said Jules. "After the kind gesture that Sarah and Tracey just made, are you not going to give Damien his case back?"

"Am I bollocks! I won this fair and square. His skinny shite probably won't fit me, but it'll still be better than spending ten days sitting in my own skidmarks. No, sorry, but he'll have to get over it like a big girl."

Damien clenched his fists and felt his stomach knot up. Danni placed a hand on his back and rubbed. "Don't let him get to you. I'm sure this is just some big prank by the producers."

Chris headed off to the bedroom, wheeling Damien's trunk behind him like a treasure chest. Damien stared daggers into the man's thick back every inch of the way until he was completely out of sight.

Damien shook his head and huffed. *It best be some kind of prank, because I don't know how much more of this I can take.*

6

Damien needed every ounce of self-restraint he possessed to keep calm whilst he watched Chris saunter around in his trainers. He knew the guy was only doing it to get a reaction. It wasn't worth taking the bait.

Damien knew Chris's type well. They thought that by provoking a reaction and trying to intimidate people, everyone would just assume they were genuine hard men and back off. The truth in most cases, however, was that those with the most 'swagger' had the least to back it up with. Their overly-aggressive manner was a facade designed to win fights without them ever starting. If anybody ever actually called a bully like Chris out on his bullshit, he would probably crumble like a piss-soaked sandcastle.

Damien was sat on a stool in the kitchen. He took a deep breath as he tried to turn his thoughts to matters other than wanting to chin Chris. Aggression was not the answer, Damien's older, wiser friend, Harry, would often say to him. Violence was for fools, he would comment with a knowing look in his eye. Harry had made his feelings on criminal behaviour very clear on that long ago evening when he'd offered Damien a lifeline, a way out of his then worthless existence. Harry had stated firmly that Damien's prior thuggery and criminal behaviour would not be tolerated if he was to offer his help. Damien had agreed to change his ways, had wanted to in fact. He was glad for Harry's help.

And so Damien had trained as a master carpenter, working with Harry every single day and setting up a business. At first, Damien had been excited at the potential to make an honest living, to even strike it rich, but that had quickly died away when Harry insisted on giving most of their profits away to charity. Damien had cried bloody murder when half his pay cheque went to help an old people's home replace their central heating. Over time, though, he started to see the good that his hard work was doing. The act of charity became deeply satisfying – more satisfying than spending the money he gave away would have been. Despite everything Damien had ever believed about himself, and about life, he was happy to give his money away to those who needed it more. Charity had not just changed Damien's life – it had changed him as a person. It gave him a clear perspective and unburdened his soul. Previously he had felt like a pack mule, carrying his many sins around his neck and walking an endless, dusty road. Now he was a galloping horse, surrounded on all sides by wonderful green fields. He had been set free.

And Harry was to thank for it.

And now it's he who needs the charity. After all of the people Harry has helped over the last few years, he deserves to have somebody help him. I'm going to make sure that person is me. I need to pay him back for all that he's done for me.

"Don't let Chris wind you up," said Danni, sitting on the stool beside him in the kitchen. She was wearing a different top now, lent to her by Jules. The two women were about the same size, only Danni had longer, and nicer, legs.

"I'm not letting him get to me," said Damien, probably unconvincingly. He could hear his teeth grinding between words.

"Good. Because it's probably best not to mess with that guy."

Damien huffed. "It's not Chris that's worrying me."

"Then what is it? What are you worried about?"

He looked at her and then looked away. "I'm more worried about me and what I might do to him."

"HOUSEMATES, ASSEMBLE IN THE LIVING AREA. VOTING IS ABOUT TO COMMENCE."

Damien stood up with Danni and went over to the sofa to join the other housemates. Chris nodded at Damien from over by the couch. He lifted up one of his trainers and rested it on his knee.

Just ignore him. The only thing I should focus on is staying in the house longer than him. That's how I'll beat him.

Everybody sat down on the sofa, backs erect, ready for what came next.

"ALL HOUSEMATES MUST NOW CONDUCT A VOTE FOR WHOM THEY WISH TO UNDERTAKE THE HEAD TO HEAD ELIMINATION. AS LEADER OF THE WINNING GROUP IN TODAY'S TASK, JADE IS EXEMPT FROM THE VOTE."

"Sound!" said Jade with a catlike grin on her face. She pointed to Damien and nodded. "We'll start at this end of the sofa and go along one after the other."

Damien sighed. He hadn't expected to go first, and was uncomfortable having to name someone openly – not that he had any problem with choosing the 'who' or the 'why'.

He decided to just get it over with. "I vote for Chris,

because I don't like him. I don't like him at all."

Chris sneered at Damien, but Damien refused to make eye-contact. The big guy had it in for him anyway, stealing his luggage and flaunting it around the house, so it wasn't like he had just made a new enemy.

Although it's worrying that the producers let a sociopath like him in with the rest of us.

Next up was Alex. "I vote for Damien," he said quickly, "because I feel that he lost us the task earlier."

Damien sighed. It was a fair enough answer. Perhaps he *was* responsible.

Jules voted for Chris. Damien had the feeling it was in support of him.

Jade voted for Jules. It seemed like it was in defence of Chris. Alliances were definitely forming.

Sarah voted for Danni because she thought the other woman was 'a little bit cold.' Lewis sided with her and voted for Danni too.

Catherine voted for Damien because 'he didn't join in last night and drink with everybody else.'

Richard voted adamantly for Lewis. He didn't explain why.

Patrick voted for Chris and, surprisingly, voiced his dislike of the man being because of him not handing over the luggage to its rightful owner like Sarah and Tracey had. Damien nodded at the older man in appreciation.

Least somebody is on my side.

Tracey voted for Danni for the same reasons as Sarah. That just left Chris to vote. No mystery as to who the man would vote for.

"I vote for Damien," Chris said, "because the guy swigs diet coke and spends his time in the kitchen like a poofter."

Damien laughed it off. The guy was an absolute jerk, but

perhaps it highlighted the errors in Damien's game plan. It was only the first day and people were already voting for him. He would not win the prize money if it continued.

"HOUSEMATES, THE VOTING IS NOW COMPLETE. DAMIEN AND CHRIS BOTH HAVE THREE VOTES EACH. THEY WILL COMPETE AGAINST EACH OTHER IN THE HEAD TO HEAD ELIMINATION TASK. THE LOSER WILL BE REMOVED FROM THE COMPETITION."

Chris blew Damien a kiss. "Just you and me, little lady. Can't wait!"

And he calls me *a poofter?*

Damien said nothing. He wasn't going to waste his breath talking trash with an imbecile. Whatever happened, one of them was leaving the house very soon, so there was no need to tolerate each other much longer. Certainly no need for a confrontation.

"DAMIEN, CHRIS, PLEASE ENTER THE ELIMINA-TION CHAMBER. THE OTHER HOUSEMATES CAN WATCH YOUR PROGRESS VIA THE LIVING AREA'S VIEWING SCREEN."

Damien stood up and walked towards the door. A moment later, Chris overtook him and bumped him aside with his shoulder. Damien scowled.

Bloody wanker!

The two of them stopped in front of the door marked ELIMINATION CHAMBER; the one that had been previously locked.

"Is it open?" Damien asked.

Chris tried the handle and it turned. He stood aside as the door opened. "Ladies first."

Damien huffed and shoved his way through the door. Inside was a stark white room that hurt his eyes with its brightness. There was no furniture or fixtures of any kind. The space was an empty cube.

Except for a small table in the centre of the room.

The steel table was on wheels, like the kind of thing you saw on forensic cop shows next to a dead body during an autopsy, usually with a whole host of bloody tools on it. This one, however, held only a pair of pistols. Damien stared down at the handguns with concern. Chris went to pick one up, but The Landlord's voice interrupted him.

"ON THE TABLE IN FRONT OF YOU ARE TWO BB GUNS. THEY ARE LOADED WITH PLASTIC BALL BEARINGS AND ARE NON-LETHAL. HOWEVER, PLEASE REFRAIN FROM AIMING THEM AT ONE ANOTHER. DOING SO WILL RESULT IN DISQUALIFI-CATION FROM THE TASK."

Chris winked at Damien. "Might just be worth it," he said.

There was a whirring sound and a compartment on the back wall opened up. A pair of marksmen targets appeared inside. Damien relaxed as he started to understand the task ahead of him.

It's just target shooting, nothing sinister.

Then The Landlord said something which confused Damien all over again.

"YOUR BRACELETS CONTAIN ENOUGH NEURO-TOXIN TO KILL YOU A HUNDRED TIMES OVER. YOUR NECK COLLARS CONTAIN A COUNTER-AGENT."

Chris's eyes narrowed and his shoulders hunched up. "The fuck he just say?"

"I don't know," said Damien, unsure if he'd just heard correctly. "It must be a wind-up."

"IN ONE MINUTE YOUR TASK WILL BEGIN. EACH TIME YOU HIT THE TARGET ON THE OPPOSITE

WALL, YOU WILL RELEASE NEUROTOXIN INTO YOUR OPPONENT'S BLOODSTREAM WHILE RELEASING THE COUNTER-AGENT INTO YOUR OWN."

"The hell are you talking about?" Chris shouted at the ceiling. "Nobody is putting anything into my bloodstream. Let me the hell out of here."

"FAILURE TO PARTICIPATE WILL RESULT IN EXPULSION FROM THE HOUSE."

"Fine," said Chris. "EXPEL ME. I QUIT."

There was silence in the room. Chris looked around anxiously. Damien expected men in the eyeball-logo jumpers to come piling in any second to remove them.

But no one appeared.

Then Chris cried out.

Damien stared at the other man. "What is it? What's wrong?"

Chris's entire face was beetroot red and drool spilled from the corner of his mouth. A vein throbbed on his forehead.

"Jesus," said Damien, rushing over to help him. "They're poisoning you. They're actually doing it."

"It...*burns!* I feel like I have fire in...in my veins." He scratched at his wrists around the bracelets like a heroin addict seeing imaginary spiders on their skin.

Damien spun around in a circle, looking for an exit or something to help, but the room was closed on all sides. "Stop this," he screamed. "Stop this right now."

Chris's agony continued to grow. The man dropped to his knees and bellowed in agony. He sounded like a wounded bear.

Damien took shallow breaths as he tried to think of something he could do. But how could he do something when he didn't even understand what was happening?

Then he had an idea.

Damien picked up one of the BB pistols and aimed it at Chris's target. He pulled the trigger rapidly, missing with every shot, but gradually adjusting his aim. Finally a ball bearing hit the target. It flashed green and let out an audible *ping!*

He fired several more times until Chris's bellows of pain became shallow whimpers.

He's getting better. The counter-agent is working.

But then Damien was struck by an unbearable pain. It started in his wrists and seemed to shoot right up into his skull. His chest went tight and his stomach distended. He dropped to his knees and began panting. His fingers seized up, locking the BB pistol in his hand.

"Help...help me," he begged Chris.

Chris had risen back to his feet unsteadily and, while still in obvious pain, he seemed to be doing much better. His cheeks had lost their redness and the vein in his forehead had stopped throbbing. He went over to the table and looked down at the remaining gun.

"That's it," Damien said. "You need to shoot my target. I need the counter-agent."

Chris looked down at Damien and nodded as if he understood. He picked up the gun and raised it towards Damien's target.

Yes, that's it. God, please hit the target.

Then Chris adjusted his aim and fired several shots upon his own target.

More burning hot agony flooded through Damien's wrists. He cried out for mercy, but Chris continued to fire at his own target.

More of the neurotoxin entered Damien's veins.

He felt himself dying. It wasn't a feeling of fading or slipping away, but more an immense pressure building to a crescendo that would ultimately reach a breaking point and end his life.

Damien collapsed onto his side.

He's going to kill me if he keeps firing.

God...it hurts so bad.

Damien realised that there was only one way to stay alive. He raised his BB pistol up, tried to aim it, but his hand was shaking. Tremors wracked his entire body.

He managed to fire the pistol, but got nowhere near the target.

Chris's target *pinged* and went green again.

Damien's agony increased.

He gritted his teeth and tensed every muscle in his body. He fought with everything he had to keep his hand from shaking for just one single fleeting second while he aimed.

Just...need...to...keep...still....

Aim...carefully...

He squeezed the trigger slowly.

The gun fired.

Then fired again.

Both shot's hit the target, lighting it green. *Ping! Ping!*

Damien felt a pinch in his neck as the counter-agent entered his system. He felt better immediately. The tremors stopped. The pain in his muscles subsided.

He rose gingerly to his feet, breathing deeply to deal with the lingering pain, but knowing he had to move fast if he had any chance of staying alive.

Chris continued firing wildly and managed to hit the target again. Damien's agony increased but he ignored it, pushed it out of focus. He took careful aim at his own target and let off another three shots. Two of them hit. *Ping! Ping!*

Chris cursed loudly. His face was growing beetroot

again. He continued firing his pistol rapidly, but was now shaking too much to hit the target.

Damien aimed carefully again, taking his time, controlling his breaths. He let off two more shots. Both hit.

Ping! Ping!

Chris screamed in agony and fell down to his knees. He placed his pistol down on the floor and put his hands up in surrender. "I give up. Please, Damien, stop. I'm sorry, just don't fire anymore."

Damien took his finger off the trigger. He looked down at Chris and wondered how the guy had ever seemed so imposing. He was just a trembling mess now, whimpering on the floor like a wounded kitten.

Damien lowered the pistol to his side and looked up at the ceiling. "Landlord, this game is over. Chris quits, so let us out of here."

"THE TASK WILL END WHEN ONE OF YOU IS DEAD."

Damien shook his head. "Are you insane? You can't just kill people for...what is this anyway, entertainment?"

"THE TASK WILL END WHEN ONE OF YOU IS DEAD."

"Then you'll have to kill me. I won't be responsible for taking another man's life. Not even a snivelling piece of shit like Chris."

Chris leapt to his feet and roared. The BB pistol was back in his hand. "Screw you, bitch!" He fired his weapon at Damien, again and again and again.

Something sharp bit Damien's left eye, sending him spiralling to the ground in shock. He cried out as half his vision suddenly disappeared.

Oh shit, oh shit. I'm blind.

Chris continued to fire the pistol, the ball bearings

bouncing painfully off Damien's skull as he covered up as much as possible.

There was a hiss and the targets on the wall disappeared back behind the sliding panels from which they had appeared. The Landlord came back over the speakers.

"HOUSEMATE, CHRIS. YOU WERE INFORMED THAT AIMING YOUR PISTOL AT YOUR COMPETITOR WOULD RESULT IN DISQUALIFICATION. HOUSE-MATE DAMIEN IS THE WINNER."

Damien was still on the floor, clutching at his eye as it wept an ocean of salty liquid down his cheek. He needed a doctor. The damage could be severe.

Chris continued aiming the pistol at Damien and was snarling like a mongrel. "You piece of shit," he shouted. "You don't deserve..."

Chris's voice trailed off as his eyes went unnaturally wide. He dropped to his knees and began wheezing. His red face now went a deep purple and blood vessels began to break apart in his eyes. Damien watched in horror as the man's nose exploded in a torrent of blood and he collapsed face down on the floor like a beached whale.

"Jesus Christ. Chris, are you okay?"

Chris didn't move.

Behind Damien, the door to the living area reopened automatically.

"YOU ARE FREE TO JOIN THE OTHER HOUSE-MATES, DAMIEN. CONGRATULATIONS ON WINNING THE FIRST TASK."

Damien remained on the floor for a while. He was panting and moaning in pain as the counter-agent took its time doing its job.

Congratulations? A man is dead.

What have I got myself into?

7

Damien stumbled out of the Elimination Chamber and fought the urge to vomit. Everybody stared at him with wide, unblinking eyes as he re-entered the living area. Behind him, the door to the white cube room closed on its own and locked.

"Please tell me that was all one big joke," cried Jules. She pointed to the large television screen. "What we just saw isn't real, right?"

Damien shook his head. He wanted to say something, but there were no words that could adequately explain or even make sense of what had just happened. His one eye was still closed and he might be partially blind, but even that, right now, seemed inconsequential.

"What happened in there?" Jade asked. For once, her voice was softer and less sure of itself. She folded her tattooed arms around herself tightly, almost as if to stop herself from shaking. A cigarette burned down to the nub between her fingers.

Damien moved over to the sofa just as his legs failed him. He dumped down against the cushions and lay back.

He shook his head over and over, and didn't blink for what must have been several minutes.

"Is Chris really dead?" Tracey eventually asked him. "Did they really just poison him?"

"Course they didn't," said Richard. "No bleeding way."

Damien looked at them all, making eye-contact with each of them in turn, and then said, "They killed him. I know that for sure, because they almost killed me. Whatever is in these goddamn cuffs is lethal."

There was a frightened squeal from one of the group, but Damien didn't see from whom. What he did see was the ashen, terrified expressions of his companions.

"This can't be happening," said Jules. "It makes no sense at all."

"No, it doesn't," Alex agreed. "Why would they kill Chris?"

Damien shook his head. "I don't know, but I think one thing is for sure – none of us is on television right now. This whole thing must have been some kind of scam."

Everybody groaned as the reality of the situation sunk in. Jade had already gone and grabbed a bottle of red wine and was now gulping from it loudly.

"So, there's no prize money?" said Sarah.

"What a crock of shit," said Tracey. "The money was the only reason I'm here."

Richard hissed at her. "Bitch, that's the least of our worries."

"Don't call me that."

"Then don't act like a bitch."

"There's no point falling out with one another," said Danni. "We have to figure this out together."

"Figure what out?" Richard flapped his hairy arms like a flustered bird. "We're stuck in the middle of God-knows-where with a madman injecting poison into us whenever he feels like it! We're screwed; totally effing screwed."

Damien had a headache and his wounded eye had begun to throb. The older lady, Catherine, seemed to notice his discomfort and sat down beside him. "Let me take a look," she said.

Damien allowed the woman to prod her fingers around his cheek and then slowly ease his eyelid open. The pain wasn't too bad, but the tears were unending. It was like a faucet had been turned loose inside of his eyeball.

"Can you see anything at all?" Catherine asked him.

"It's all blurry."

"That's okay, blurry is good; better than seeing nothing at all. I think you're going to be okay. Your eye is pretty inflamed, but it doesn't seem like any permanent damage has been done."

Damien sighed with relief. "Thanks. I hope you're right."

The old woman smiled at him. "Well, I'm not a nurse – just a care worker – but I think it looks okay."

"You're a care worker?"

Catherine nodded and her glasses bobbed on her wrinkly nose. "I was. Retired last year. I was hoping to win myself a nest egg to grow old on. Guess that isn't going to happen now."

"Can we concentrate on something a little more important than his fucking eye and your career, please?" said Richard. "Like how we're going to stay alive."

There was a sudden flashing that made all of them turn around. The large television screen was alternating between bright green and dark red. The flashing was so rapid that Damien was sure it would trigger an epileptic seizure in those who suffered from the condition. Then the flashing stopped and the familiar logo of the staring eye appeared.

A video began to play.

An elderly gentleman in a worn, grey suit and a bright red dickey bow appeared onscreen. His milky eyes held back tears. "My...my son, Graham, supported the Baggies his entire life, ever since I took him to see his first game at The Hawthorns. We used to live in Smethwick back then and could walk to the matches. It kept us close, you know? Going to see the match every two weeks gave us a bond that not every father is lucky enough to have with his son. I miss those days." The old man began to cry silently. Tears trickled down his weathered cheeks but he continued speaking. "My son was a grown man with children of his own when that vicious thug killed him at the train station. Graham always used to feel guilty for leaving his family on a Saturday to come watch the football, but it was time with his old dad; he wouldn't sacrifice it. I loved him for that. He grew up to be such a kind man – a man I was proud to have raised."

Someone off camera handed the old man a tissue and he used it to wipe at his eyes. "That wicked monster stamped my son's skull into the pavement, just because he was wearing a West Brom shirt instead of an Aston Villa one. That was it, the only reason. The wretched beast had a few beers before the match, came out the pub, and decided it would be fun to kill my son. And what did he get for it? Four years." The old man spat on the floor in disgust. "He said my son had started the fight and that the killing was accidental. The drunken louts he was with backed up his story. But I know it isn't true. I know my son." The old man stared hard into the camera. "And now I'm going to be the one having fun watching you die, Christopher Maloney. I hope you rot in Hell you thug."

The television screen went blank.

Alex ran his hands through his blond hair and whistled. "What the hell was that?"

Danni put a finger to her lips. "Shush," she said. "Something else is coming up on the screen."

Sure enough, a new image appeared on the high-def screen. It was a grid of silhouetted faces – three squares by four – twelve people in total. The first silhouette slowly transitioned into a full colour photograph. It had been taken recently. It was Chris's dead face, taken from inside the Elimination Chamber where Damien had left him.

"Oh God," said Jules, covering her mouth with the palm of her hand. "Oh God, oh God."

More images began to appear onscreen. This time it was a collection of words. Beneath Chris's photograph the word THUG began to blink. It was what the old man had called him.

Below the other featureless silhouettes – unclear even in their gender – were the following words: COWARD, CHEAT, MURDERER, ABUSER, WHORE, TRAITOR, TRICKSTER, PEDDLER, PREDATOR, CRUSADER, and finally the word, THIEF.

"What the hell is going on?" Richard demanded of no one in particular.

"I don't know," said Damien. "But I think we're in a lot of trouble."

DAY 3

I t had been difficult to fall asleep for obvious reasons. Chris's death, and the inexplicable situation they had all found themselves in, had quickly led to panic. Each of the housemates had tried to force the metal bracelets from their wrists, even going so far as to draw blood as they fought desperately to wrench their hands through the unforgiving steel rings. Damien had worn the flesh almost down to the bone in an attempt to remove his own shackles. But it did no good. They had all searched desperately for a way out of the house. But it did no good. They pleaded and begged to be released. But it did no good. Eventually they had all succumbed to the weariness and fatigue of their shocked minds and given up completely.

Since then the housemates had huddled together on the large sofa, afraid to separate. Jules had snuggled up against Damien and he had let her, understanding the woman's need for comfort. He needed it himself.

Now that the sun was rising and a new day approached, Damien felt afraid for the first time in years. Would they still be forced to continue with this sick and twisted game now that they were no longer willing? Would there be more tasks and more votes? Would he have more to worry about than a wounded eye?

Now that he'd had a few hours' sleep, his eye had almost returned to normal. It was sensitive and weepy, but the pain was mostly gone and he could see through it again. He'd been worried for a while and was glad to have his full sight back. He could think of nothing worse than losing his sight, or even just part of it. But, now that it was clear it would be okay, there were other things to worry about.

We need to find a way out of here.

First I need to find out why we're even here, though. This isn't just random bad luck. Chris was killed in revenge by someone who knew him. The old man wanted him here.

Is this all just one big grudge?

But who would have a grudge against me?

Damien's mind was reeling. While he had not always lived a good life – far from it in fact – he considered himself to be a good man. Any enemies that he had were deeply buried in his past, and that's where they should stay.

But sometimes forgotten enemies are the ones who bite hardest.

There was no one that came to Damien's mind as a likely perpetrator for his recent predicament, so he decided to focus on other things for the time being – and right now that was food. If he and the other housemates were going to have any chance of getting through the next seven days, they would need their strength. They would all think more clearly with food in their belly.

Damien pulled himself up off the sofa and padded quietly to the kitchen. No one else was awake yet due, once again, to the fact that they had all drank too much. Now, more than ever, Damien was glad for his sobriety. Anything could happen inside this house and he wanted to be ready for it – not drunk and in denial.

They're acting like if they just get drunk enough it will all go away.

They need to get their heads out of their arses.

Damien headed over to the kitchen cabinets and pulled out some boxes of cereal. He lined up a handful of bowls and began pouring in the corn flakes. He finished it off with a pint of milk from the fridge. He had expected to eat alone, but Danni woke up and joined him.

She took the stool next to him at the counter and grabbed one of the bowls of cereals. Damien handed her a spoon.

"Get any sleep?" he asked while adjusting his collar to get at an itch.

"A little bit. It's not very easy to relax right now, you know?"

"You don't have to tell me." He took in a mouthful of cereal and suddenly considered it strange that his tormentors had even bothered to provide fresh food and drink. If they were all in the house to be killed, what did it matter if they were fed or not?

"You think they'll make us do another task later?"

Damien nodded. "I think this whole thing has been set up to punish us. I felt the poison in my wrists. It was real. These people aren't playing around. I can only imagine the planning and cost that would have gone into keeping us all here."

Danni nodded, stared into her cornflakes and mixed them around with her spoon. "So you think we're pretty much screwed then?"

Damien swallowed a lump in his throat and sighed. "I really don't know, but I don't intend on giving up. Once everyone is awake, we'll keep trying and find a way out. There must be something we can do."

"I hope so, because I don't want to die here. I didn't want Chris to die either, even with what he'd done in his past."

Damien looked at her for a moment and felt his mind wander. "You mean that man he killed at the train station?"

Danni nodded.

"I was thinking about that. It was obvious the old man wanted revenge. That was why Chris was here. You think that's why we're all here?"

She looked at him as though she wasn't following. Her dark eyes went narrow. "What? You mean we're all here because someone wants revenge against us?"

"Yes."

"In that case, what are *you* guilty of?"

Damien thought about it for a moment, scanning back through the mental filing cabinet of his past memories. "I'm guilty of a lot of things," he admitted. "But nothing that I deserve to die for. If somebody thinks any different then I intend to meet them face to face so I can find out why."

"Well," said Danni. "All I'm worried about right now is not getting voted for. I don't know what I'll do if I have to do a head to head elimination like you did last night. I'll be as good as dead."

Damien placed a hand on her arm. He didn't want her to be afraid. She would be better off focusing on the present. "You'll be fine," he said to her. "We can all surprise ourselves when our backs are up against the wall. We'll find a way out of this, I promise."

Danni smiled at him, but there were tears glistening in her eyes. "Partners?" she said.

Damien nodded. "Partners."

8

Everybody gathered in the garden. They seemed to feel less trapped out there; like they were somehow freer if they could keep the open sky in their view. It was a little warmer today and the sun gave off a sliver of warmth.

The large camera above the staring eye kept watch on them all.

Damien knew that the real reason they were all gathered together in a group was because they were waiting for whatever came next. They knew that the nightmare was not yet over – only just beginning in fact – and they were all dreading the sound of The Landlord's voice.

I wonder who he is. Is he a maniac? Or does he have a motive for what he's doing to us?

Damien looked up at the grey sky and put the time at about mid-day. That was when the booming voice they had all been waiting for finally came over the speakers.

"HOUSEMATES, PREPARE FOR TODAY'S TASK. IT WILL COMMENCE IN FIVE MINUTES."

"Oh God," said Jules. "Oh God, Oh God."

"Just calm down," Jade chided her. "I'm not going to have you fucking this up."

"Fucking this up? What am I doing?"

"Nothing," said Jade. "But if you end up on my team, I won't have you freaking out and losing me the task."

"Just back off Jade," Damien warned. "None of us are the enemy here."

"No," said Jade. "You're just the competition; only now the prize is getting out of here alive."

"None of us is getting out of here alive," said Alex. "We're as screwed as a kid at Gary Glitter day care."

"Just be quiet," said Tracey. "You're not helping anyone by stating the obvious."

Their bickering was interrupted by a motorised whirring. The hidden platform in the garden – the one that had contained glass compartments yesterday – was rising up out of the ground again. This time it did not contain glass containers. It contained a metal table with several sets of pliers. There must have been some sort of preparation area below where someone was able to change around the equipment on the platform.

"HOUSEMATES, YESTERDAY CHRIS WAS ELIMI-NATED FROM THE COMPETITION. THE PRIZE MONEY OF TWO MILLION POUNDS IS STILL UP FOR GRABS. NOW MORE THAN EVER YOU MUST PARTICIPATE IN THE TASKS AHEAD. YOU ARE COMPETING NOT ONLY FOR THE MONEY BUT FOR YOUR LIVES."

"Why are you doing this?" Jules shouted at the raised platform as it were a conscious being. "Why are you doing this to us?"

"BECAUSE YOU DESERVE IT. EACH OF YOU HAS WRECKED LIVES IN PURSUIT OF YOUR OWN SELFISH DESIRES. YOUR SINS WILL BE EXPOSED.

YOUR ONLY SALVATION WILL BE BY SURVIVING UNTIL THE END. ONLY THROUGH THE BLOOD OF YOUR COMPETITORS WILL YOU FIND ABSOLUTION."

"This is insane," said Alex. "You'll pay for this, whoever the hell you are."

"I AM NO ONE. I AM JUST A FACILITATOR FOR JUSTICE, A SERVANT OF THE SCALES."

"You call this justice?" said Damien. He had heard enough. "I've spent the last years of my life helping people and giving to charity. You think you are *just* by trying to kill me? I am guilty of nothing."

"ALL ARE GUILTY. YOUR ACCUSERS ARE REAL. YOU WILL PERFORM THE TASKS. THE ELIMINATIONS WILL CONTINUE."

"Screw you," Damien said. He sat down on the floor and crossed his arms. "I won't play your sick games. Poison me if you have to, but I promise you I will die with a clean conscience."

"YOUR OBEDIENCE IS NOT REQUIRED IN THE TASK TO FOLLOW, HOUSEMATE DAMIEN. THOSE WHO SUCCESSFULLY COMPLETE THE FORTHCOMING INSTRUCTIONS WILL WIN IMMUNITY FROM TONIGHT'S VOTE. THEIR LIVES WILL BE PROTECTED FOR ONE MORE DAY."

Damien remained seated on the floor. He was not going to be a puppet. Whoever was behind all of this would undoubtedly kill them all anyway, so why play along? If he was going to die, he would rather it be sooner than later.

"HOUSEMATES, YOUR TASK IS AS FOLLOWS. PICK UP THE PLIERS ON THE TABLE BEFORE YOU. REMOVE THREE FINGERNAILS. DO THIS AND YOU WILL BE SAFE FOR ANOTHER DAY. FAIL AND YOU RISK BEING

PLACED IN TONIGHT'S HEAD TO HEAD ELIM-INATION."

Everybody let out a groan as they digested what they had just been asked to do. Jules looked like she might vomit and had gone deathly pale.

Damien stood up and went over to her. He placed an arm around her trembling shoulders. "Come on," he said. "Sit down on the ground with me and take some deep breaths. You'll end up panicking otherwise."

Jules nodded and did as she was told, sitting on the grass. "Would you blame me for panicking?" she said. "This is a nightmare."

Damien looked her in the eyes and made sure he held her gaze before speaking. "No. This isn't a nightmare. This is just the sick game of a psychopath. The less we cooperate, the less power he has. Don't make the mistake of thinking he is anything more than a man."

"He might be just a man," Jade said. "But right now he's giving us no choice. I'm not going to die in here." She marched forward, over to the table on the platform. She picked up a pair of pliers and turned around to face the group. Her chest heaved in and out as she took several deep breaths.

Then she placed the pliers against her little finger and clamped down hard. She grunted, yanked and twisted, then let out a sharp yell as her manicured fingernail tore away from the sticky flesh of her nail bed.

She screamed. "SHIIIITTTBALLS! Wow...that hurt like a mother!"

"You need to pull two more," said Alex, wincing as Jade held her bloody nail up in the nose of the pliers.

Jade took a few more deep breaths, seemed to mumble something under her breath, and then quickly clamped down on her engagement finger. She tore the nail free quickly and growled with the pain. A series of dry heaves took over her and she had to take deep breaths to keep from vomiting. She was sweating badly. Agony etched itself into the lines of her face.

The final nail Jade tore free was from her middle finger. She screamed again, louder than ever. It looked like she might pass out, but instead she put down the pliers and simply said, "I'm going to go get a drink."

"JADE IS IMMUNE FROM THIS EVENING'S VOTE. CONGRATULATIONS, HOUSEMATE."

"Bite me," she said as she left the garden on wobbly legs.

Damien remained sitting on the floor with Jules. She was leaning up against him now and trembling.

"I'll go next," said Alex.

"I think I can do it, too," said Richard. "Especially if a bird managed it."

Damien watched as the two men got to work with the pliers. They hissed and cursed as they tore their nails loose from their fingertips. They immediately grew pale and looked near to passing out. If anything, the two men seemed to find the task much harder than Jade had. They were close to tears by the time they were done. Alex's nose dripped snot and his eyes streamed tears.

"ALEX AND RICHARD ARE IMMUNE TO TONIGHT'S VOTE. CONGRATULATIONS."

"Think that drink sounded like a good idea," said Alex. "Come on, mate."

The two of them went after Jade. The relief of the task being completed was clear on their faces. They could relax now, at least for the next twenty-four hours.

Damien looked around at the other remaining house-mates. Lewis and Sarah and Tracey were in a huddle and discussing something between themselves. It didn't seem like they had any intention of using the pliers. The same seemed true of Patrick, who walked off without a word and re-entered the house. Catherine went right behind him.

That just left Danni, Damien, and Jules. Danni looked down at Damien on the floor and smiled. "I'm with you. If I'm going to get tortured and killed, the last thing I'm going to do is make it easy for them.

"Oh, God," said Jules. "They're going to vote for me. I'm going to end up having to do something even worse, like Chris had to. I'm going to die."

"Calm down," said Damien. "We're all going to stick together and get through this."

Jules pulled away from him. "No, we're not. The maximum number of people that can get through this thing alive is two – and that's only if they split the prize money. There're three of us here right now, so at least one of us – but probably all of us – is going to end up dead. I'm weak. I won't make it."

"Just calm down."

Jules sprung to her feet. "No! I can't go in a head to head elimination. I can't!"

She ran over to the table and picked up a pair of pliers. Damien got to his feet and followed after her, although he kept his movement slow, not wishing to add to her panic.

"Get back," she said, pointing the pliers at him. "I have to do this."

Damien wanted to stop her, but he also knew that if she went through with it, she would be safe and, as such, would calm down.

Jules put the pliers against one of her fingernails and yanked. She screamed out in pain. The nail had torn in half with a shard still attached to her cuticle. Damien winced as she dived in again with the nose of the pliers and clamped down on the nail and a sliver of bleeding flesh. She yelled even louder this time, as she yanked a chunk of her nail bed out along with the nail. Tears streamed down her cheeks, but she continued on. She looked up at the sky and screamed. "Is this what you want, you sick fuck?"

She yanked her pinkie nail free in one go. Then her engagement finger. Then her middle finger. Then her thumb nail.

"Hey, stop," said Damien. "You've done it. Stop hurting yourself."

Jules carried on ripping free her nails. She managed to take off her index fingernail by the time Damien made it over to her and tore the pliers free from her hand.

He pulled her in tight as she sobbed and bellowed in agony. She convulsed in his arms as the pain wracked her. Then her knees folded and she crumpled to the floor and vomited onto the grass.

"Okay," said Damien. "It's over now. You're safe. You were strong and no one can vote for you. You were strong."

Jules just sobbed.

The camera and the giant eyeball watched them with indifference.

Danni came over to them both and knelt down. She placed a hand on Damien's back and rubbed up and down his spine. "She might be safe, but let's just pray that no one votes for us tonight."

Damien sighed. He didn't believe in God, but right now he wished he did. Because praying felt like a good idea.

9

D amien retrieved his luggage, seeing as how Chris no longer had any claim over it. He swapped his jeans for a pair of tracksuit bottoms and swapped his button-up shirt for a warm hoodie that hid the collar around his neck. He felt far better and much readier for any physical challenges that might lie ahead. But he also felt unclean. It had been more than seventy-two hours since he'd last washed and there was nowhere, other than the house's single toilet, where one could conduct any sort of personal hygiene. He considered using the sink in the kitchen or maybe trying to wash up in the hot tub if things got much worse – which invariably they would.

As he sat alone in the garden, Damien contemplated once again why he was in the situation he was in. Primarily it was because he had volunteered in order to win the prize money – which was still up for grabs by the sound of things – but he was also sure that none of the housemates were there by random chance. They had all been chosen for some reason.

The smart-suited gentleman that had visited Damien

and Harry's wood shop several weeks ago had obviously not been a 'television producer' looking for 'ordinary people' to compete in a game show. It was obvious now that Damien had been targeted and mislead. Whether or not that man posing as a producer knew how much Damien had needed the money was unclear. Perhaps it was just a grim coincidence. Perhaps not. Damien would not have even considered entering the house if circumstances were different.

The other housemates would probably all have similar stories of how they had been convinced to be there. He wondered if the man in the suit had been The Landlord, or just someone working for him.

The biggest question on Damien's mind, however, was *who* would want him punished? Who would want to enact revenge against him? He had never killed anybody like Chris had, had never wrecked anybody's life, at least to his knowledge.

Maybe those words beneath the silhouettes on the television screen are the answer.

He thought about some of those words now. *Murderer – was that one meant to be Chris? No, the one beneath Chris said 'Thug'.*

So does that mean another one of the housemates is a murderer?

There were also the words *Predator, Traitor, Peddler,* and several others. Damien had no clue which word was meant to apply to him. None of them as far as he was concerned.

They must have the wrong guy. I shouldn't be here.

"HOUSEMATES, PLEASE GATHER IN THE LIVING AREA."

Here we go again.

Damien went and joined the others inside. They had all assembled on the sofa. There was a thickness to the air that was equal parts unwashed sweat, cigarette smoke, and palpitating fear. Damien felt his own heart beating fast with anticipation.

One of us will likely be dead within the hour.

"HOUSEMATES, PLEASE VOTE FOR WHO YOU WISH TO PARTICIPATE IN TONIGHT'S HEAD TO HEAD ELIMINATION TASK. JADE, ALEX, JULES, AND RICHARD HAVE IMMUNITY AND CANNOT BE VOTED FOR."

Once again, Jade started the voting. "Damien."

"I vote Damien, too," said Alex. He shrugged his shoulders. "Sorry."

Damien rolled his eyes. Everybody seemed to be voting the same as they did yesterday. Nothing had happened for anybody to change their minds about anything.

"I vote...Sarah," said Damien, picking pretty much at random. He didn't want to condemn anybody to death.

"I vote Sarah, too," said Danni.

"Why?" Sarah asked, apparently hurt.

Danni stared at her. "We haven't been asked to give a reason, but it's because you hang around with Lewis and whisper whisper whisper. I think you're working on your own little game."

"So are you," Sarah rebuked. "I vote for you!"

"I vote for you too," said Lewis.

Danni chuckled. "See? There's my point."

"I vote Damien," said Tracey.

"I vote for Sarah," said Jules. "Same reason as Danni.

Catherine surprised everybody by voting Lewis. She said they had nothing in common, which seemed like a pretty mundane reason considering the situation.

Patrick jumped on Jade and Alex's bandwagon and

voted, "Damien," while Richard finished off with a vote for Lewis, same as last time. Again, he didn't explain why.

"Hey, man," said Lewis. "Why you always be voting for me?"

Richard shrugged his shoulders. "Because I like you least. Isn't that the point?"

"But why don't you like me?"

"Why do you care so much? We're all strangers here."

"HOUSEMATES, YOU HAVE VOTED. DAMIEN AND SARAH WILL COMPETE IN THE HEAD TO HEAD ELIMINATION TASK."

"No!" Sarah screamed. "I won't go in that room and play your evil games." She suddenly bolted, dodging furniture as she sought a way out. She fled to the garden, scurried across the grass courtyard and leapt against the far wall, clawing at it as if she hoped to climb it through will power alone. The other housemates hurried out after her, calling out for her to calm down. As she jumped up at the wall, trying to drag her way up with her fingernails, her feet slipped out of her heels and left them strewn across the grass.

"Calm down, sweetheart," said Lewis. He approached her from behind slowly. "You're going to be okay."

Sarah spun around and faced him. Her eyes were wide and feral, bleary with tears. "I'm not going to be okay. They have us locked up in here like animals in a slaughterhouse. If I go into that room to do the task, I won't make it out again."

"You don't know that," said Lewis. "You might be the winner. Damien might be the one who dies."

Thanks, thought Damien.

"And you think that's okay?" Sarah cried in disbelief. "What then? Even if I win, that won't be the end of it.

There'll just be another vote. Who knows what sick, twisted games they have waiting for us. I can't do this."

"You don't have a choice," said Jade. "We're playing for our lives here. If you give up then you're dead for sure."

"It's okay for you, Jade. You're a bitch. You won't think twice about screwing someone over in order to win. I don't have that in me."

"Hey, fuck you," said Jade. "I'm trying to help you. I won't bother next time, but you're going in that room whether you like it or not."

"I will not!" Sarah turned back around and began scrabbling at the brickwork again.

Lewis reached out a hand to her. "Darling, there's no way out of here."

She spun around to face him again, only this time she shoved him aside and marched back across the courtyard. She re-entered the house with the other housemates in tow. No one knew what she was planning to do, but it held their rapt attention like an ensuing train wreck. They were all happy for her to try and escape, if only to see what happened.

Funny how everyone is content to be a spectator, until it's their turn. Then they lose their minds. Nobody was panicking when it was me in there.

Sarah headed over to the kitchen. She was clutching at her mousy blonde hair with both hands and letting out a breathy moan. Madness had taken over her and with each second that passed she seemed to descend more and more into a mental abyss where any rational thought was absent.

She opened one of the kitchen drawers.

"What are you doing?" Damien asked, suddenly getting a bad feeling.

Sarah pulled out a curved knife and pointed it at the

housemates. They all kept their distance behind the counter as she shouted at them. "Stay back," she screamed. "Just stay back."

"Hey," said Danni. "Calm down, sweetheart. We'll figure something out. I...I'll take your place. Okay?"

"Don't be stupid," said Jade. "You're talking about your life, Danni. You can't volunteer to go in her place. This is a competition and she has to play by the rules."

"I don't care," Danni said. "I've had enough of this."

Tracey shrugged her shoulders. "Just let her. What difference does it make?"

Sarah laughed, but it was a hysterical, unhinged noise. "You hear that?" she shouted at the ceiling. "You here that, Mr-fucking-Landlord? She's going to take my place. She's going to do the task, so leave me alone."

There was silence for a moment.

Then the speakers crackled.

"UNNACCEPTABLE, HOUSEMATE SARAH. YOU WERE VOTED FOR BY YOUR PEERS. YOU WILL PARTICIPATE IN THE TASK."

"No, I won't." Snot and tears were now streaming down Sarah's puffy face. The knife in her hand wobbled.

"Come on," said Lewis. "Give me the knife, darling. We'll figure something out."

She shook her head at him and seemed finally to get a hold of herself. She took a deep breath and stopped shaking. "I won't go in there," she said in a slow whisper.

Then she ran the knife across her wrist below the steel bracelet.

Blood jetted down her arm and dripped in a steady stream from her fingertips. She stared at them all with a look of child-like wonder in her eyes. She almost seemed to smile for a moment. Perhaps she was glad to have made her own decision, instead of being forced into something she didn't want to do.

Then her legs buckled.

Lewis tried to grab Sarah, but he wasn't quick enough and she crumpled to the tiled floor. The rest of the housemates stood around in shock while she slowly bled to death on the kitchen floor.

10

On the television screen a silhouette changed to a picture of Sarah. Unlike the one taken of Chris this was a personal photo taken from a previous time. It was a photo where she was smiling. Beneath the silhouette was the word THIEF.

A video started playing.

A withered old lady appeared onscreen. She looked tired and frail, perhaps in her final year. When she spoke, her voice sounded like rustling leaves.

"When I met George, my best days were behind me. I was forty-nine years old and divorced. I didn't think I would trust a man ever again. But when I met my George, I had no choice but to fall in love with him. He was a kind man, a funny man; worked hard every day of his life without a single complaint. I loved him from the start. I loved him completely. His daughter, though, that was another matter. She only came by when she wanted something – money usually. When I married her father she made no secret that she did not approve. She acted like her father was somehow betraying her mother, but the woman had been dead gone nine years – a tragic car accident, God bless her soul. George still loved her of course – I never resented him for that – but he also loved me. He provided for me and made me happy. We had twelve wonderful years together.

Then he got cancer. Sixty-six years old with only a year to live. I cursed God for giving him to me for such a short while. I had wasted so much of my life before I met him, and now I was going to lose him. But I was thankful for the time we still had together.

We took a trip to Australia while he was still well enough and then came home to spend our last months together. I retired from work and spent every day with him. When the time finally came, he told me about his will, told me he was leaving everything to me and that I would be looked after. I forgot about it for a while, focused only on spending as much time as I could with my George. I was never interested in his money.

He lasted another week and then passed away in a fit of pain. I'll never forget his last, agonising hours. It haunts me to this day.

I found the will a couple of weeks later amongst the things in his office. As he had said, it left everything to me, with the exception of a small sum which I was to give to his daughter, Sarah. Even though she had barely visited her father while he was ill, I was happy to honour my George's wishes. I invited her to the house and went through the will with her. She was angry to receive so little. She said that I had forced him to sign it all away. She stormed up to the guest room in a huff and didn't come back down again all night.

The next day the will was gone and so was Sarah. As I hadn't married George – our previous failed marriages had been enough to jade us towards the institution – Sarah was able to contest my claim towards her father's assets. She got everything apart from the house, which the court's awarded to me after having lived there and paid bills for twelve years. George had left almost two-hundred thousand pounds to me, but it all ended up going to Sarah. She took it with a smug smile on her face the whole time, even though she knew that her father's final wishes were being ignored."

The old woman let her pale lips stretch into an ugly scowl. She shook her head and looked off camera. "I couldn't afford to run the house on my own so I had to sell it. It was the only part of George I had left. At first I was going to use the money to place myself in a nice little nursing home, but I decided that without my George there was little point being 'comfortable' as my life was already over. I opted to go into a state care home, where the conditions are of course much poorer. I've been here for more than ten years now. I'm an old woman; a lonely, bitter woman. But I kept the money from the house for a rainy day. I'm finally putting it to good use.

I hope the money was worth it, Sarah, because this is the price you are paying for your selfish ways. You were a bad daughter to your wonderful father and I hope that when you die, you go to a far different place than him."

The screen went black. The silhouettes reappeared. Ten shadows were left. Ten words yet to find owners. The THIEF and the THUG were dead. Who would be next?

11

I t had taken a good part of an hour for Sarah to die. The blood that pumped from her wrist seemed to go on forever. They tried to staunch it, by wrapping her arm tightly with a belt from Damien's luggage, but it had only delayed the inevitable. The tourniquet was just a band aid on a deep and critical wound.

During this time, while Sarah lay dying on the floor, not a single person had tried to enter the house. No one had offered medical attention or even acknowledged the incident at all. Now, more than ever, the housemates realised that someone wanted them dead and that no help was coming. All they had now was each other, and yet they were also enemies in a game that had become about life and death.

The only reason the cameras were there was to capture their suffering.

Nobody knew what to do with Sarah's body so they left her on the kitchen tiles for the time being. Lewis seemed the most upset by her loss, but only marginally. Obviously, there was only so much they could care about one another after only a few days. It was clear that Lewis had lost an ally, though, and right now allies were extremely valuable.

"HOUSEMATES. DUE TO SARAH'S EARLY ELIMINATION FROM THE HOUSE, THE NEXT MOST VOTED-FOR HOUSEMATES WILL PARTICPATE IN THE HEAD TO HEAD TASK. ALONG WITH HOUSEMATE DAMIEN, BOTH LEWIS AND DANNI WILL NOW COMPETE. PLEASE STAND BY TO ENTER THE ELIMINATION CHAMBER."

"That ain't fair," said Lewis.

"Just deal with it," said Richard. There was a smirk on his face. "Everybody gotta go sometime."

Lewis glared at him. "Dude, what is your goddamn problem with me?"

"I just don't like people like you."

"People like me? What...you mean because I'm black?"

Richard leant back against the rear of the sofa and smiled calmly.

Lewis shook his head and sighed. "Man, that ain't cool. Maybe you didn't get the memo, but the world moved on."

"Don't talk down to me, nig-"

Lewis squared right up to the bigger man. "Now I know you weren't about to say what I think you were about to say."

Richard laughed. He wouldn't look Lewis in the eye, almost as if he couldn't bear to.

Lewis stiffened. "Look at me, you racist piece of shit."

Richard shoved Lewis away from him and then swung his fist. He punched Lewis on the jaw and sent him reeling to the ground. Less than a second later, the larger man was stamping on Lewis's head. Over and over again.

The sound was sickening.

Damien leapt across the room, tackling Richard to the ground and climbing on top of him.

Richard looked up at Damien and grinned. "My problem ain't with you, brother, so get the hell off me."

Damien shook his head in disgust and got up off the man, but he made sure to stand between him and Lewis. Lewis was lying on his side, dazed and moaning. A trickle of blood flowed from the corner of his mouth and from his nose.

Damien glared at Richard, but the man seemed proud of his actions. "You're a real piece of work, you know that?"

"Just looking out for my country. Apes and ragheads have no place in a Christian land."

"You're no Christian," said Danni. "You're a goddamn caveman."

"You'll thank me one day, sweetheart. If we let them take over then we'll be speaking monkey and living in holes in the ground by the end of the decade."

"HOUSEMATES, THE DOOR TO THE ELIMINATION CHAMBER IS NOW OPEN. DAMIEN, DANNI, AND LEWIS, ENTER IMMEDIATELY."

Lewis was still on the floor and moaning. Jules was crouched down beside him, trying to rouse him.

Damien looked up and addressed The Landlord. "We need a minute. Lewis is hurt."

"ENTER NOW OR YOUR BRACELETS WILL ACTIVATE. ALL THREE OF YOU WILL DIE."

Damien huffed and looked at Danni. She seemed equally as frustrated. "This is ridiculous," he said. "Come on, let's try and carry him inside. We'll help him through it."

They went and grabbed Lewis under the armpits. They managed to get him up into a sitting position when they saw that his left eye was bloodshot and closed over – either from Richard's fist or from his stamping boot.

That guy is going to pay for this.

With an awkward heave they managed to get Lewis on his feet. Thankfully he was conscious and managed to stand more or less on his own, but he was extremely groggy and disorientated. They had to steer him towards the door at the far end of the living area to keep him from wandering off.

"I'll get the door," said Danni, leaving Damien to hold onto Lewis on his own.

"Racist motherfucker," Lewis mumbled, leaning his weight against Damien. "Gonna...gonna kick his ass once I get this over with. Once I get this over with. Once I... Gonna kick his ass once I get this over with."

Damien looked at Lewis and noticed that the guy's pupils were different sizes. Damien was no doctor, but he guessed it was concussion or maybe something even more serious. Whatever damage had been inflicted by Richard's beating would no doubt affect Lewis's performance in whatever task lay ahead of them. It was totally unfair.

But neither Danni nor I are responsible. We just have to do whatever it takes to save our own backsides.

I'll do my best to help him, but whatever happens to Lewis is beyond our control.

Danni held the door open and Damien helped Lewis pass through it. Once again Damien was faced with the stark-white cube room. Chris's body was no longer there. Someone had obviously come and moved him.

A clean-up crew.

How many people are working here? Just the guys in the eyeball jumpers? Or are there more? What about the guy in the black overalls? Is he The Landlord?

In the centre of the room this time was a large iron casket, standing upright and about six foot high. The front of the casket was heavily rusted and had an opening in the middle about the size of a sheet of A4 paper. There seemed to be something inside, attached to the back wall.

"HOUSEMATES, THIS IS A TOTAL ELIMINATION TASK. IT IS ALL OR NOTHING. IF ALL OF YOU SUCCEED, ALL OF YOU LIVE. IF ALL OF YOU FAIL, ALL OF YOU DIE."

Damien exchanged a glance with Danni. The chance that they all might live was somewhat of a relief, but the ominous cabinet in the middle of the room gave them little cause for hopeful thinking.

Lewis didn't even seem to realise what was going on. He was slumped up against the wall by the door they had entered through. He was muttering nonsense to himself.

"HOUSEMATES, YOUR TASK IS TO PRESS THE BUTTON AT THE BACK OF THE CABINET. IT IS THAT SIMPLE. GOOD LUCK."

Damien stared into the hole of the cabinet and noticed the big red button inside. It was no different to the emergency buttons you found at the bottom of escalators to halt them during an accident.

"We just have to press the button?" said Danni. "Seems a little simple."

Damien breathed out through his nostrils. "Yeah."

Then a whirring sound filled the room and they all saw the true nature of the task. Inside the casket, a pair of metal fan blades began spinning in opposite directions. They passed rhythmically over the gap in the middle of the casket, making access to the button perilous if ill-timed.

Danni groaned. "God, we're going to lose our arm if we stick it in there."

"Not necessarily," said Damien. He was paying close attention to the *whomp whomp* of the passing blades. "They're not spinning that fast. There's perhaps a second –

maybe a little less – where the gap is clear. If we time it just right, we should be able to press the button and get our arm back out before the blades catch us."

"I'm sure it's not as easy as you make it sound."

Damien took a long swallow. "I'll go first."

He approached the casket and the spinning blades. His eyes fell on the thick rust stains that surrounded the enclosure, but he quickly realised that they were something else.

Bloodstains!

Does that mean that people have been here before? Have there been other victims going through this in the past?

What is this place?

Damien could feel the cool air rushing from the blades. *Whomp whomp whomp!*

He took a deep breath and tried to sync his inhalations and exhalations with the spinning of the blades. He was still sure that there was a brief window between each crossing where a person could get their hand in and out.

He breathed in.

He breathed out.

In...

Out.

In...

Out.

Whomp whomp whomp.

Damien inched his hand closer. Close enough that he could feel the vibrations of the air on his fingertips. The button at the back of the closet seemed tantalisingly close. The task seemed so simple. But the timing was imperative.

Whomp whomp whomp.

Breathe in....

Breathe out.

His fingers inched closer.

Come on. I can do this. Just pay attention to the blades.

Whomp whomp whomp.

Damien jabbed his hand forward like the head of an uncoiling viper. His fingertips hit hard against the rubbery plastic of the button.

He yanked his arm back.

Whomp!

The fans continued spinning. Damien's arm was still attached. He was panting like he'd just run a marathon.

"CONGRATULATIONS, DAMIEN. YOU HAVE PASSED THIS TASK."

Damien took in a relieved gasp of air. "Thank God for that."

"Guess, I'm next," said Danni. By the nervous twang of her voice, it was clear that she was not confident.

"Just take a few seconds and get the timing right," Damien told her. "You can do this. Just take some deep breathes and watch the blades."

Danni shook her head and smiled. "I'll do my best."

Damien took a look at Lewis while Danni stepped up to the casket. "Hey, man," he said. "You got to snap out of whatever daze you're in. This is serious."

Lewis looked at Damien, but his eyes were not focusing at all. "I got this, man. Don't....don't worry about me...about me."

Damien sighed and turned around just in time to see Danni shove her hand into the gap and press the button.

Whomp!

She turned around and faced him, a great big smile on her face. She flapped her arms excitedly. "I did it. *Fuck*, I did it."

Damien nodded and smiled. "Good going. See, I told you that you could do it."

"What are we going to do about him?" Danni motioned towards Lewis who was still slumped up against the wall and bleeding.

"I don't know," Damien admitted. "He's totally out of it."

"HOUSEMATE DANNI, YOU HAVE SUCCEEDED AT THE TASK. HOUSEMATE LEWIS, PLEASE PROCEED TO THE CENTRE OF THE ROOM. YOU MUST MAKE YOUR ATTEMPT."

Without argument Lewis staggered away from the wall and approached the casket. From the blank expression on his face, he was either extremely confident or did not understand what he was doing.

"Be careful," Damien told him. "You have to time it just right."

Whomp! Whomp! Whomp!

"I got this!" Lewis said cockily, but there was a slight slurring to his words.

He's on another planet. I don't think he knows what he's doing.

Damien and Danni exchanged a worried glance and then watched Lewis make his attempt. He moved his hand forward slowly, a little bit at a time. It seemed like he understood the danger and was being cautious. Damien was relieved.

Maybe he might just do this.

Then Lewis wobbled drunkenly on his feet and fell against the casket. His arm went into the hole. He didn't bring it back out again.

Blood arced into the air. It filled the room in a fine mist and spattered Damien's face.

Lewis tumbled backwards and began giggling. His right arm was missing from just below the elbow and a jagged shard of bone jutted out of the stump. The blades inside the casket were stained red and making a grinding sound as the bracelet from Lewis's severed wrist rattled around inside it.

Danni turned around and gagged.

Lewis continued giggling as some kind of shock response flooded his system with euphoric hormones. He suddenly lost the ability to stand and crumpled to the floor as though his skeleton had turned into custard.

Damien dropped down beside Lewis and urgently placed his hands on the bleeding stump of his arm. The blood came thick and fast.

"What do I do?" Damien cried. "I can't stop the bleeding"

"Do nothing," Danni said, shaking her head and sighing. "There's nothing you *can* do."

"HOUSEMATES DAMIEN AND DANNI, PLEASE EXIT THE ELIMINATION CHAMBER. THE TASK IS OVER. CONGRATULATIONS."

Damien gazed down at Lewis. The guy was still giggling but the sound was becoming weak and pitiful. He was fading fast.

"We can't just leave him."

Danni took Damien by his arm. "There's nothing you can do. Come on."

Damien allowed himself to be led out the room. When the door locked behind him, he couldn't help thinking: *Three down. Nine to go.*

12

On the television screen, one of the silhouettes changed to a picture of Lewis's dead body. The word TRICKSTER was written beneath it.

A new image appeared on screen. It seemed to be some sort of rap sheet, like the ones police kept on criminals. In the top left corner was a photograph of Lewis with thick dreadlocks and a goatee. He looked like a different person – only the eyes were the same. To the right of the photo was a list of crimes: **Counterfeiting Notes & Coins, Forgery, Fraud by False Representation, Internet Fraud, Conspiracy to Obtain Money Transfer by Deception.**

A news report began playing. It featured a stern-faced police officer standing behind a pedestal and addressing a forest of microphones.

"Mr George Ochonogor is responsible for crimes amounting to many millions of pounds, obtained via confidence tricks and several internet-based deceptions often referred to as 419 scams. However, I am happy to report that a large part of that sum has been recovered. The suspect is, however, still at large. Mr Ochonoger is a master of deception. He has a fluent grasp of many accents, most notably from the regions of Manchester, London, Birmingham, as well as his natural Nigerian dialect. He has lived in the country now for over a decade and has become naturalised with a keen ability to blend in. During that time Mr Ochonoger has been responsible for the destruction of many lives. The people he has stolen from demand that he be made to pay for his crimes. If anybody has any information, please come forward."

The video finished playing.

13

Jade and Tracey were pretty drunk. They had necked perhaps four bottles of wine in the last few hours. It had also been noted that the wine they'd drunk on previous nights had been replaced with new bottles and a carton of cigarettes.

"Why are they feeding us and giving us booze?" Jade slurred. "If they're just gonna kill usssh."

"Probably to keep us docile," said Richard as he sipped from a beer can and puffed on a fag. "Make us all drunk and stupid."

"If you think that," said Danni. "Then why are you drinking?"

"Because there's naff-all else to do, sweetheart. Only thing a man likes to do is drink and fuck."

"Speak for yourself," said Damien.

Richard grunted. "What's climbed up your arse? You look right pissed off."

"Why do you think that is?" said Danni. "Lewis is dead because of you. If you hadn't of stomped on his head he might have had a chance of doing the task. I hope you saw what you did to him, you wicked man."

Richard smiled. "Oh, I was watching, sweetheart. I watched every second. I enjoyed watching that bloody mongrel get put down like the animal he is. If I ever get to meet The Landlord, I'll have to shake his hand."

"You're a piece of work. A man is dead and you laugh and insult him?"

"An animal is dead. You all saw what his crimes were. He was a parasite, just like the rest of them."

"Makes me wonder what your crimes must be," said Danni, narrowing her eyes at him. "I bet it's worse than anything Lewis ever did."

"Sweetheart, if you don't take your beady fucking eyes off me right now, you're gonna lose 'em. I ain't guilty of nothing, so keep your goddamn trap shut."

Damien picked up his glass of water from the table and took a very slow, very long sip. Then he placed the empty glass back down on the table with a soft *clink!*

"Richard," Damien said calmly. "I want you to listen very carefully to me, okay?"

Richard just raised an eyebrow at him. The man seemed amused, yet slightly apprehensive.

Damien took a slow breath in through his mouth and let it out through his nostrils. "I am going to say this just once, Richard, so I hope very much that you will listen. I am not a violent man, not at all, but once upon a time I'm afraid that I was. In fact, I was one mean little tracksuit-wearing, drug-snorting, beat the shit out of you and your friends, mother-fucker. Lucky enough for you, Richard, I decided to change my ways and live a peaceful existence. I have a good friend to thank for that; he showed me the light. Tonight, however, I am willing to make an exception. You see, if I hear one more tiny, piddly, microscopic morsel of racist, sexist, disrespectful rubbish spew forth from your ignorant fucking mouth, I am going to punch you in your windpipe so hard that all you'll be able to do, while I stamp your skull into the ground like an orange, is cry out for your ugly mother."

Richard smirked defiantly, but Damien could tell that the man's confidence was rocked. His cocky, self-assurance had been unbalanced. His testicles were shrinking. Damien couldn't let the little peanuts recover.

"Now, you might be thinking to yourself that I am just making an empty threat, that my bark is worse than my bite. That's why I'm asking you, right now, Richard, if you do not believe me, come and try me. Come over here and I will tear you apart like wrapping paper at Christmas. I will make you part of the carpet. Because you see, you racist piece of shit, I will beat you so bad that your goddamn soul will be bruised. They'll have to bury you in a coffin full of Tupperware containers."

Richard went to speak but Damien waved a hand.

"Richard, if you want to see how sharp my teeth are, just open your mouth one more time. That's all it's going to take."

Richard's eyes narrowed. His lips kept moving as if he was unsure whether or not to speak – whether or not to answer the challenge. Eventually he just got up from the sofa and took his beer and cigarette away with him into the garden.

All of the other housemates stared at Damien with wide, unblinking eyes. He knew their looks well. It was the expression of fear and respect. It was a look he used to get all the time on the Birmingham council estates.

Guess I still got it.

He leaned back against the sofa and took a deep breath.

His knee was shaking and he could feel the adrenaline coursing through his system. What he was feeling was something he loathed and constantly fought to keep at bay, so much so that it sometimes made him feel nauseous. It was a thirst for violence.

Yet, as much as he hated it, God did it feel good.

DAY 4

Damien had decided to take up one of the rickety beds in the bedroom across the garden. He'd chosen it last night, right after he had helped Alex drag Sarah's body from the kitchen over to a spot at the far corner of the courtyard. Everybody wanted her body as far away as possible. Jules and Danni had cleaned up all the blood from the tiles.

The mattress on which Damien now lay was ripped, its springs digging at his back, but it was still a bed; just being in one made sleep easier. It was a ritual the body needed. It was still unclear why The Landlord had provided the house-mates with only six beds, but Damien imagined it was just another way of breaking their will.

Besides Damien, only Alex, Jules, and Danni chose to sleep in the bedroom. Jade, Catherine, Richard, Tracey, and Patrick slept in the living area on the sofa. Two groups had formed and Damien reluctantly accepted that the other group was closer-knit than the one he was a part of. Alex, for example, had voted for Damien twice now, and Jules was skittish and likely to do whatever was best for her. Ironically, the only person he trusted at all was Danni; the one who had said from the beginning that they should be partners, that they were the *same*.

I just hope I get a break from the head to head eliminations. I'm not sure I can take another one.

"You awake?" Danni whispered from the next bed over. She was clutching at her metal collar and trying to scratch at the aggravated skin beneath.

"Yeah. I've been awake a little while, just thinking."

"Me too. I have no idea what time it is. I think it's almost midday."

Damien sat up on the bed and rubbed sleep from his eyes, adjusted his collar and bracelets. Scabs had formed underneath. "I think that, too. There'll be a task to do soon."

Danni groaned. "Can't wait. Wonder what sick torment will be imposed on us today."

"Come on, guys. I don't want to think about it." It was Jules speaking from another one of the beds. "My fingers are killing me after what I had to do yesterday. The pain has kept me awake all night. Don't think I can go through any more torture. I certainly can't cope getting voted into a head to head tonight."

"Maybe you won't have to," said Danni.

"What do you mean?" Jules asked.

"Well, if we all agree to vote for another member of the group, we should be okay."

"Not necessarily," said Alex, the final member of their group joining in the conversation. "There's always at least two that go into the head to heads. We would only be able to vote one person in. The rest of them would probably be voting for one of us. Plus we don't know who will be immune yet."

"Well, okay," said Danni. "I suppose I'm just trying to make the point that we can help our odds a little."

"I like the idea," said Jules. "Who would we vote for?"

"Dunno, who would you like to?"

"Jade, maybe? Or Richard. He's pretty horrible."

"It's not fair to conspire," Damien said.

Alex huffed. His blond hair was fanned out like a peacock. "And you don't think they're planning against us?"

"Exactly," said Danni. "I think we should all vote Richard. After what he did to Lewis, we can't risk having him in the house any longer. He could attack one of *us* next."

"I sorted the Richard problem out," said Damien. "He got the message."

Danni shrugged. "You don't know that. He might just be thinking things through; planning a way to take you out. You were pretty harsh to him last night, not that the pig didn't deserve it."

"Okay," said Jules. "I'm going to vote for Richard."

"Me too," Alex agreed.

"And me," Danni added. "How about you Damien? You with us?"

Damien looked at them all, absorbed their apprehensive stares, and then allowed himself to be convinced. As much as he didn't like it, he accepted that this was how the game would have to be played. He didn't want to face another head to head. It was somebody else's turn.

"Okay," he said. "We'll vote for Richard."

14

"HOUSEMATES, PLEASE GIVE YOUR VOTES."

"I vote for Richard," Danni said immediately, following the plan they had made earlier in the bedroom.

"Me too," said Alex.

Richard scowled at him. "Big mistake, little man. You better hope I don't come back out."

Alex fiddled with his tie nervously. "It's nothing personal, Richard."

"The hell it isn't."

"I vote for Richard too," said Patrick. "You can threaten me all you like, young man, but you won't frighten me."

Richard huffed. "We'll see about that, Grand dad."

Damien was surprised to see someone on the 'other team' voting for one of their own. Perhaps they were not as close knit as he'd believed. Patrick seemed, at the very least, to be a neutral party. The older man had also stood up to Chris, too, during the first voting session.

The guy obviously doesn't like bullies. Good on him.

Damien cleared his throat. "I vote Richard."

"Screw, you all," he said. "Vote for me, I don't give a damn. Whoever is up against me is worm food."

"I vote for Alex," said Tracey. "He clicks his fingers all the time and it's really annoying."

Alex became flustered. "What? You're going to vote for me because of a habit?"

Tracey shrugged her shoulders. "It's annoying."

"I vote for Alex as well," said Richard, beginning to chuckle. He nodded to Alex and began laughing harder. "Looks like you're about to shit your pants, mate. That's two votes for you. I fancy my chances against a faggot banker."

Alex was turning pale. "Oh, God."

Catherine gave her vote next. "I vote for Danni. I'm tired of having to stare at her legs all the time. I've never seen such short skirts."

I know what you mean, thought Damien.

Danni shrugged and seemed to take the comment in her stride.

Jade was the only one with a vote left. She used to it to seal Alex's fate.

"HOUSEMATES RICHARD AND ALEX WILL COMPETE IN TONIGHT'S HEAD TO HEAD ELIMINATION. PLEASE STAND BY."

Alex began breathing erratically, pacing back and forth.

Richard sneered at him and laughed. "That's it, mate. I would be shitting myself too. You ain't got no chance against me."

"Shut it, Richard," Damien warned him.

"Else what? You'll give me another one of your tough guy speeches. Give me a break."

Damien decided to take another tack. He went over to Alex and took the anxious man to one side. "Don't listen to him, Alex. He's just trying to get inside your head. You have as much chance of coming through this as him. Take it from a guy who has already survived two of these things. Just stay calm and focus."

Alex pulled his tie loose, unbuttoned his collar. "I can't stay calm, man. I'm shitting a brick here. What the hell will they have me do?"

"I don't know," said Damien. "Just keep your mind in the moment. You think ahead and you'll just make yourself panic."

Alex took some deep breaths and then nodded enthusiastically. The smell of sweat wafted from his pores. "You're right. I just got to go in there ninja-style and do what I have to do. No fear, right?"

"Exactly. No fear."

"HOUSEMATES ALEX AND RICHARD, ENTER THE ELIMINATION CHAMBER."

"Christ, here goes," said Alex. He took a few moments to collect himself and then clicked his fingers like a pair of guns. "Let's do this."

Richard positively swaggered over to the Elimination Chamber door. It was unlikely that the guy was completely without fear, but he was doing a good job of masking it. It was more than likely just a mind game to try and unnerve Alex. In all honesty it was a smart thing to do.

Damien sat down on the sofa in the living area and stared at the viewing screen. Everybody else took a seat around him.

"You'll be able to see everything from here," said Patrick. "We've watched your last two tasks."

Damien stared at the television as it switched from displaying the grid of silhouettes to a live video feed that was coming from inside the white cube room.

Alex and Richard were now inside. The door had closed

behind them. In front of the two men was an aluminium table with a hose attached at one end. Two pipes stuck up from the centre of the table about a foot apart.

Damien groaned. "What the hell have they got in store this time?"

"HOUSEMATES RICHARD AND ALEX, WELCOME TO THE ELIMINATION CHAMBER. YOUR TASK IS SIMPLE..."

Two gouts of flame ignited from the two steel pipes on the aluminium table.

"HOLD YOUR HAND OVER THE FLAME. WHOEVER LASTS THE LONGEST WINS. THE LOSER WILL BE EVICTED."

The sound feed coming from inside the room was crystal clear. Damien could hear everything, could hear the other men's fearful breathing. Richard even went so far as to voice his reluctance.

"You bleeding psycho. Is this how you get your jollies? You better hope we don't meet."

"HOUSEMATES, YOU MUST BEGIN THE TASK IN THREE SECONDS OR BOTH OF YOU WILL BE DECLARED LOSERS. 3...2...1...

Richards and Alex both sucked in a breath and thrust their palms over the red hot flame coming from the pipes. The flaming apparatus was not dissimilar to high school Bunsen burners, but with a far more morbid purpose.

Both men started to yell. Richard let out a manly bellow, but Alex's screams were like that of a child.

The resolution of the viewing screen in the living area was so high that Damien could see the smoke trails beginning to form. He could see the men's flesh begin to blister and boil at the edges. He could only imagine the damage being done to their hands.

Alex fell forward onto the table, but kept his hand in place. He was making animal grunting noises and stamping his feet. Richard gritted his teeth and tensed his entire body, went still like a statue. He was completely silent now and took deep, slow breaths, almost as if he were trying to meditate through the pain.

"This is sick," said Tracey. "I can smell them burning."

Damien couldn't smell anything and wondered if the woman was exaggerating or if her horrified mind had merely created the imagined odour of singed flesh.

Alex began to sag, his knees bending, his legs bowing. Sweat poured out of him in great gouts and his eyes began to roll back in his head.

Then he slumped to the floor.

Richard saw that his competitor had taken his palm away from the flame and quickly followed suit. He yanked away his own hand and backed into the nearest wall. He was snarling with pain, but also had a relieved grin on his face.

"HOUSEMATE ALEX, YOU HAVE LOST THIS TASK. YOU ARE ELIMINATED FROM THE COMPETITION."

Alex tried to get to his feet but was only able to make it to his knees. He clutched his burned raw hand against his stomach while reaching at the ceiling with his other. "No, please," he begged. "Don't kill me. Please, just-"

Alex's words were cut off. His eyes bulged. Blood escaped his nose. He clutched at his wrists desperately, but after only a few seconds, he collapsed face down on the floor. He died the exact same way as Chris, poisoned by the neurotoxin.

"CONGRATULATIONS, HOUSEMATE RICHARD. PLEASE LEAVE THE ELIMINATION CHAMBER. BANDAGES AND ANTISEPTIC HAVE BEEN PROVIDED IN THE PANTRY. PLEASE TEND TO YOUR WOUNDS.

15

The customary video, intended to condemn Alex, appeared onscreen. Everybody sat quietly on the sofa while it played. It began with the word 'COWARD' being displayed on screen.

A CCTV feed began. It was in black and white and seemed to have been recorded at night. The scene showed an empty road, a zebra crossing in the foreground.

A stranger appeared on the screen. It was a young woman. She was dressed as though she'd been on a night out, high heels and glitzy dress. She was about halfway across the zebra crossing when a long silver Mazda hit her. Fortunately the car had only been travelling at about 20mph, but that just made it even more bizarre that the driver hadn't managed to stop in time.

Then it became clear. The CCTV images showed a clearly inebriated man falling out of the Mazda. The man was undoubtedly Alex if the platinum blond hair was anything to go by. He was wearing a crumpled suit and had party streamers hanging from his neck. He'd obviously been at some sort of do; perhaps some opulent function arranged by the bank.

Alex stared down at the woman on the ground and shook his head in obvious horror. The victim was badly injured, but still conscious. She reached out to Alex weakly.

He continued staring down at her for a moment longer.

Then he got back in his car and drove away.

The CCTV video feed ended and a young woman in a wheelchair appeared on screen. A huge divot of missing flesh scarred the left side of her face. She was smiling, but the expression was ugly. When she spoke she sounded manic. "I was pregnant, you bastard. But I found you. Ha! I found you, you bastard. I know who you are, *Alex Strickland*. Now you're going to pay."

The video ended. A picture of Alex's dead face appeared amongst the silhouettes.

Another one down.

16

The mood was sombre. Night had fallen over the house like a clinging blanket. The garden outside was nothing but a black square through the window. The remaining housemates were sharing a couple of bottles of wine, but no one was hitting the alcohol as hard as before. Nobody had even spoken in the last hour or so. Even Richard was contemplative as he picked at the bandages he had taken from the pantry and applied to his severely burned hand. Nobody had offered to help him.

"We're so screwed," said Jules. "Alex was a big time banker. The people doing this to us don't care about the consequences. We're just going to disappear off the face of the earth as far as the outside world is concerned."

"Does anybody even know where we are?" Patrick asked. His skinny neck looked odd inside the large metal collar.

"We're in the middle of nowhere," Damien answered. "I looked under my hood when we were on the bus. I think we're pretty far north, in the Highlands or something."

Patrick raised an eyebrow at him. "You managed to take a look? Did you see anything at all?"

"Just hills and mud. Like I said, the middle of nowhere."

Everybody seemed to deflate.

"So even if we get away, there's nowhere to run," said Jade.

Damien shrugged. "Who knows? I doubt they plan on letting any of us get back to civilisation. They can't have us exposing what's going on here."

"What about the winners, though?" Jules asked. "They said we can still win the money. Surely they will let the winners go."

"I doubt it."

"It's still the only chance we have," said Patrick. "I'm still intending to win if I can. I don't want to see anybody else hurt, but I'm going to do what I have to; anything that means me staying alive."

"That's fine," said Damien. "Long as you can live with the rest of us being dead, more power to you."

"What choice do I have?" said Patrick. "We're all in the same boat here."

Everybody went back to being silent. There was no way around the fact that they could only live by witnessing the death of the others. It seemed like nobody wanted to converse for fear of getting to know each other. It would only make the days ahead harder.

More difficult to watch a friend die than a stranger.

Damien could sense any willingness for teamwork drain away as individual preservation became the new priority. It was no longer about avoiding the vote; it was about surviving inside the elimination chamber once your number was up.

"We should try to escape," said Tracey. "I would rather die fighting than let someone order me around like a play toy."

Jade shook her head. "If we start trying to get out they'll just switch our bracelets on. They could kill us in seconds."

"If we all try to escape," said Patrick, "we will end up dead. At least if we play the game two of us might live. Or maybe even just one, but that's better than none."

Damien kept thinking about the notion of escaping. It was a pretty pointless pursuit, but something kept tickling at the edges of his mind, a thought trying to find its way to his brain.

He stood up from the sofa and went over to the kitchen. While he was still trying to grasp the thing that was niggling at him, he looked around at the cupboards and appliance. He wasn't quite sure what he was looking for but his gaze settled on some old egg shells and a carton of milk. An empty bottle of wine lay on its side on one of the counters.

That was when it occurred to him.

The alcohol. They've been restocking the pantry. They even left bandages and anti-septic in there for Richard earlier.

As Damien thought about the housemate's recent movements, he became certain that nobody from the outside had entered the house, which meant that the only way they could restock the pantry was if they did so from outside.

There must be a door at the back of the pantry. There has to be for them to keep filling up the room with alcohol and supplies.

Damien turned his gaze slowly to the pantry door. He wondered if he was being watched right now, recorded by the unseen cameras that must have adorned the many corners of the house.

Slowly, he inched towards the pantry, letting out a soft whistle to try and act like he was just killing time and going through his thoughts. He started to think about his next move. Even if he found a secret doorway, it would likely be locked. Even if it wasn't, he was still at a massive disadvantage due to the toxic bracelets clamped around his wrists.

Still, like Catherine said, I think I would rather go down fighting. If I can take a few lumps out of my captors then all the better.

Damien positioned himself in front of the pantry door and placed his fingers around the handle. He pushed down and pulled the door open carefully.

"What are you doing?" Danni called over to him.

Damien flinched and spun around. He realised that his heart was beating fast. He had to talk slowly in order to remain calm. He gave Danni a smile. "Just looking for some snacks," he said.

"We've put them all in the cupboards. What do you fancy?"

"I erm...was just looking if there was anything else. They might have restocked us."

"I checked a little while ago," said Jade. "But you can grab us another bottle of wine if you'd like."

Damien nodded. "Will do." He turned back to the pantry. The door had closed when he spun around, so he opened it again and looked inside. Other than a few crates of beer and several bottles of wine and some liquor, there was nothing inside except for empty space. He examined the cramped area, searching for a doorway or hatch. All he found was smooth walls on all sides.

His head dropped. He let out a sigh.

How the hell are they getting into the pantry if not through a door or hatchway?

As Damien's gaze fell to the floor, he spotted something. The bottom of the pantry was carpeted. The raggedy beige pile went from the doorway up to the back of the closet-like space. On the left and right of the floor the carpet curled up against the skirting board, but at the back of the closet it did not – it was flat. The reason it remained flat was because it went right under the wall and continued to a space beyond. The wall at the back of the pantry was not a solid structure. It had been placed down on top of the carpet.

It's a partition. Maybe they just slide it away or pull it back from the other side.

Carefully, hoping that the cameras were not picking up the inside of the small room, Damien rapped his knuckles against the partition wall. It rattled and vibrated. It was not secure.

Without thinking about the consequences, Damien rocked back and kicked out as hard as he could. The partition skidded backwards along the carpet and then fell flat with a *whomph* of air escaping from underneath.

Damien wandered into the secret room and had no time to react as the man in black overalls struck him in the face. He tumbled into the wall and tripped over the tangle of his own legs. He slid down to the floor, looking up to see that he was in some kind of storage room. There was a heavy, steel door at the far end.

The man in black overalls hopped forward and booted Damien in the chin. "The game isn't over yet, son! So you're going to get your ass back in that house and play along."

Damien spat blood and scowled up at the man. "Fuck you! I'm done being your bitch. You want to kill me, do it now. Tell whoever arranged this to go suck off a tramp because that's all they're good for!"

The man in black overalls took a run up and swung another kick at Damien's face. Damien managed to tumble aside and avoid the blow. With the other man off balance, he scrambled up to his feet and got himself some space to fight back.

He put his dukes up and spat some more blood onto the carpet. "Come on then, fuckface. Let's see how hard you really are."

The man in black overalls glared at Damien and then came right at him.

Damien fought dirty. He faked a wide hook with his right, but jabbed out with his left and struck the man in the throat, who immediately stumbled backwards, choking and spluttering.

Damien lashed out again and kicked the man's legs from under him, sending him crashing onto his back, now winded as well as choking. Damien stood over him, ready to put the man down for good. "You ain't shit, *son*," he said, raising his foot ready to stamp.

Pain shot through Damien's wrists. He staggered sideways and then fell to his knees. There was fire in his veins. The bracelets had activated. His body was being flooded with the toxin. He clawed at them, ripping off a layer of skin.

This is it! They're going to kill me.

Least I got a few digs in.

The man in black overalls hacked and coughed, caught his breath. He climbed back to his feet and grabbed a hold of Damien's collar. He began dragging him along the floor like a bag of sand.

Upside down, Damien's head fell back and he saw the other housemates standing in the entryway he'd created when he'd kicked down the partition wall.

"Get back inside the house now!" The man in black overalls shouted at them all. "Or you will all be dead in less than one minute."

To Damien's disappointment, the other housemates all complied. They scampered back inside and allowed the man in black overalls to drag him through the pantry and into the kitchen.

"Why are you doing this?" Danni whimpered.

"Shut up. Everybody go and sit on the sofa."

Damien moaned as he was harshly dumped on the tiled floor of the kitchen. The man in black overalls stared down at him and shook his head. "You just made a big fucking mistake."

The man in black overalls left.

Damien lay on his side and moaned. Danni leapt up from the sofa and came running over to him. She knelt down beside him. "Are you okay? Did they poison you?"

"Y...yeah, but I think I'm okay. The pain is going away. They must have activated the collar."

Jules had come over, too, and was staring at Damien with worried eyes. "What did you do? What just happened?"

He sat up and caught his breath. "I found a secret compartment. I didn't think about it, just tried to get through."

"But didn't you think that they would just use the bracelets to control you?"

"Of course I did, but I didn't care. I wanted to do something to fight back."

"I'm sorry we didn't do the same," said Catherine. "Perhaps that was our only chance."

"What could we have done?" Patrick asked. "Nothing, that's what."

"Would have been worth trying."

"No point talking about it now," said Richard. "It's done."

Feeling a little better, Damien managed to climb up onto his feet. He stumbled forwards but caught himself on the kitchen counter. He held himself there as he addressed the rest of the group.

"These people deserve to pay," he told them. "Whatever any of us has done in the past, nobody has the right to judge us outside of the law. Whoever is running this show is obviously getting rich by hosting some sort of revenge-a-thon. While you might not admit it, I'm sure some of you can probably work out who has placed you here?"

Everyone averted their eyes and shifted nervously on the spot.

Damien nodded. "Right, well, whether we admit to it or not, there is still a murderer, a predator, a peddler, a crusader, a whore, a traitor, an abuser, and a cheat here. We have all been bought and paid for. Do you really think they're going to let the winner go? What about the person that paid to see their death? Do they get a refund?"

"Who cares?" Richard said, bashing his hand down on the counter and wincing as he realised it was his burnt one. "We can't do anything. We try to take a shit without their approval and they can kill us dead. These bleedin' bracelets..."

Damien nodded. "I know. We are in a bad situation. All I am asking you to do is to seize an opportunity if one presents itself. If you get a chance to fight back, take it. That's what I did. At least now I can die knowing that I kicked that pussy's ass. Even more satisfying is that he knows I kicked his ass, too. Even if only for a few minutes, I took back the power they had over me."

Danni blew air into her cheeks and then let out a chuckle. "Alright, Damien. If I have a chance to scratch their eyes out, I promise I'll take it."

"Me too," said Tracey.

"And me," said Jules in a quiet whimper.

"Don't have to tell me," said Jade. "I would have done that anyway. These wankers have it coming to them."

Catherine and Patrick didn't speak, they both just nodded.

Richard stared at Damien for a long time. It started to become uncomfortable but then he finally decided to speak. "For once I agree with you. I got a lot of respect for what you just did. Pity you didn't kill the bastard."

Damien huffed. "Believe me, I was only seconds away."

"HOUSEMATE DAMIEN, YOU HAVE COMMITED A GROSS VIOLATION OF THE COMPETITION RULES. YOU TRIED TO ESCAPE. THIS CONSTITUTES A FAILURE TO PARTICIPATE."

Damien leant back against the kitchen counter and ran a hand through his short hair. "Then kill me. I'm done with this."

"ALL HOUSEMATES WILL BE PUNISHED. YOU HAVE EXACTLY THREE MINUTES UNTIL YOUR BRACELETS RELEASE A LETHAL DOSE OF TOXIN. YOU WILL ALL DIE."

"Goddamnit!" Richard yanked at his left bracelet, but of course it was useless. He glared at Damien. "Good job fixing it, hero. Now we're all going to die."

"Why would they do this?" asked Danni. "Their whole plan is ruined if they kill us all."

"This can't be happening," said Damien. The burden of putting his peers in jeopardy was already crushing him. "It doesn't make sense. I broke the rules, not any of you."

"Maybe your escape attempt screwed everything up," said Jade. "Maybe they can't continue with the game now that you found a way out."

Everybody fumbled with their bracelets, the conversation now over as desperation set in and doom approached. They all knew trying to get the shackles off would be futile, but the alternative was to stand there and accept death.

"HOUSEMATES, YOU HAVE TWO MINUTES UNTIL YOU DIE. IF YOU WISH TO LIVE, YOU MUST CHOOSE A SINGLE HOUSEMATE TO SACRIFICE THEIR LIVES TO SAVE THE REST OF YOU. EITHER ONE OF YOU DIES VOLUNTARILY WITHIN THE NEXT TWO MINUTES, OR YOU WILL ALL DIE."

Jules shook her head. "What? They want us to kill someone?"

Damien sighed. His empty stomach grumbled. "This is my true punishment for breaking the rules. Best way to break someone's will is to make them watch while their actions hurt those close to him. Well, I don't expect any of you to pay for my decisions. I should be the one to die."

"No way," said Danni. "You said we were going to stand up to them."

Damien headed over to the kitchen's cutlery drawer. He looked each of them in the eye. "And I hope that you do stand up to them. I already have. I can die with my self-respect intact."

"HOUSEMATES, YOU HAVE ONE MINUTE."

"What do we do?" Tracey asked.

"Nothing," said Damien. "Let me handle this." He rooted around in the drawer and pulled out a serrated bread knife. It wasn't very sharp but he thought it would do the job if he sawed hard enough on his wrist.

"You can't do this," said Danni. "We need you."

"There's nothing I can do for you. I'm obviously here for a reason; because I hurt somebody. Perhaps I deserve to die."

"HOUSEMATES, THIRTY SECONDS."

"Don't do it, Damien," Danni said.

"Screw that," said Jade. "If he doesn't do it then we all die."

"I can't watch," said Jules, turning herself away.

Damien held the knife against his wrist, just below the steel bracelet. He sucked in a mouthful of air and tried to steel himself. It was going to hurt, he knew that, but so would the toxin if it was released. He couldn't let other people die because of him.

I'm sorry I let you down, Harry.

"TEN SECONDS, HOUSEMATES."

Damien held the knife tightly and clamped down on his lower lip with his teeth.

Sod it! Let's get this over with.

There was a loud cracking noise.

Damien looked up just as Catherine slumped to the floor like a ragdoll. Her head was twisted around at an unhealthy angle and her body was totally limp.

Damien's mouth dropped open. "Wha...?"

Richard stared down at the dead old lady at his feet and snorted through his nose like a bull.

"What did you do?" Damien demanded.

"What had to be done. I'd rather have a young guy with some balls on my side than an old dear with rust on her pussy. It was nothing personal. Someone had to die and I chose the weak link. You're welcome."

"You broke her neck," said Jules, looking like she might faint. "How did you even know how to do that?"

Richard smirked like a lizard. "Two places you can learn to do that, sweetheart – prison and the army – and I've spent time in both."

"HOUSEMATES, THE COMPETITION WILL CONTINUE. THERE WILL BE NO TASKS TOMORROW."

Damien placed the knife carefully down on the counter. "You shouldn't have done that, Richard. I was willing to die."

"Tough luck. Guess I thought that if anybody is going to

risk their neck getting us out of here, it's you. Can't do that if you're dead."

"Still, you had no right."

Richard obviously didn't want to discuss it any longer because he walked away. Damien glanced down at Catherine's body and felt genuine sadness for the old lady. His reckless actions had gotten her killed and she had seemed like such a nice old lady.

Five minutes later, Damien's opinion of Catherine changed.

17

The video on the viewing screen was from a hidden camera inside an old person's bedroom. The elderly gentleman was frail and wispy beneath the rumpled sheets of his bed.

A nurse entered the room. The woman was obviously a slightly younger Catherine. She was wheeling a service tray in front of her and picked up a bowl from its surface.

Then she went over to the old man and held the bowl beneath his wrinkled chin. With a spoon she scooped out some of the contents and held it to his lips.

The old man turned his head. He did not want any.

Catherine's body stiffened and she took another scoop from the bowl. Then she rammed it into the old man's mouth, almost choking him. He thrashed and struggled on the bed, but was too frail to resist as Catherine forced several more scoops into his mouth.

Once she was satisfied, Catherine tipped the bowl into the old man's lap and walked away. The video had no sound, but it was obvious that the man was crying out in agony as the scolding hot broth saturated his bed sheets.

Catherine left the room with her trolley. She seemed to be smiling.

The video ended. The word ABUSER appeared beneath Catherine's picture.

DAY 5

Even though everybody was safe for at least a day, the tension had not gone away. The group was now down to just six – exactly half of the group they started with. The missing housemates' absence weighed heavily on those remaining. Jules had taken to crying frequently while Richard had started pacing the perimeter of the courtyard over and over.

Damien had dragged Catherine's body into the bedroom across the courtyard. He placed her on top of one of the scummy mattresses and left her alone, just like she had left the old man in the video. Her death may have been partly Damien's fault, but he didn't care. Catherine had been an evil person.

And so was everybody else that's died in here.

Does that mean that the remaining housemates are evil, too?

Am I evil?

Murderer, whore, peddler, crusader, predator, and cheat.

Which one am I? And which ones are they?

I don't know if I can trust any of them.

Damien headed back into the living area and joined the

other housemates. They had all worked together on making a stew and it was now ready. The smell of boiling beef and vegetables was mouth-watering. With all that had happened, Damien had not eaten half as much as he usually would have.

"Grub's up," said Richard, offering him a bowl.

Damien took it and went and ladled himself a portion. It was bland and rubbery. It needed salt and better meat. Still, it filled the void in his stomach and instantly made him feel stronger. He could almost feel the nutrients floating through his bloodstream.

"How you holding up?" Danni asked him.

"Better now that I've eaten."

"And at least we have the day off."

Damien frowned. "I wouldn't call it that. A reprieve maybe, but not a 'day off'."

"I'm just glad we don't have to watch anybody else die today."

Damien was curious about something, so he asked a question. "Which label on the television screen belongs to you?"

Danni was about to spoon in a mouthful of stew, but she lowered her hand back to the bowl and glanced at him. "Kind of personal."

Damien shrugged. "What's anybody got to be shy about? It seems like our darkest secrets will all be revealed eventually whether we like it or not. I'd just like to know you now while you're alive, instead of after you're dead."

"You think I'm going to die?"

He shook his head. "No, I didn't mean that. I just mean that it might be better if we confess our sins rather than have them exposed by a maniac."

Danni seemed to think about it for a moment; then she

nodded her head slowly. "You're right. I'm pretty sure that I'm the *whore*."

Damien raised an eyebrow. "Wow! I didn't expect that. You don't seem like the, ahem, *whore* type."

Danni smiled and Damien saw for the first time that she had a gap between her two upper teeth. It made her look cute and childlike. "Thank you," she said, seeming to blush. "I'm not the person I used to be – just like you said that you're not. I was married once, but it was never a good fit for me. I played around all the time. I just couldn't get enough. I don't know what it was, insecurity, immaturity. I guess both. Anyway, my husband knew that I was always sleeping around with other guys, but he pretended otherwise. I knew how much he loved me and I think he was just trying to find the best way to cope with it. I suppose he was insecure as well, otherwise he would have divorced me. Eventually I went too far."

Damien licked his lips and swallowed. "How?"

"I slept with his brother."

"Yikes! That's pretty cold."

A tear formed in Danni's eye and she nodded solemnly. "I know. But that's not the worst part. Sleeping with my husband's brother was the straw that broke the camel's back. My husband hung himself the day after he found out."

Damien shook his head and stared into her eyes. He imagined her husband swinging by his neck, alone when he spent his final moments. It was a tragic way to go. Danni seemed truly remorseful but, *damn*, if it wasn't a terrible thing she had done. Although Damien hated the existence of such a misogynistic word, *whore* was a pretty accurate way to describe her actions.

"Anyway," Danni said, wiping the tears from her eyes before they had chance to fall. "I did a lot of thinking after that; re-evaluated my life. Indirectly or not, I killed my husband – a kind and caring man. I carry the guilt with me always, but I try to harness it to make better decisions. My husband died three years ago. I haven't slept with a man since."

Damien let out a deep breath as he digested what he had just been told. As much as he condemned Danni's actions, he was in no place to judge. The man he had once been was no better than the woman she once was.

"I was a drug dealer," he admitted. "And a bully."

Danni's eyes went wide. "Really? You? But you don't even drink."

He laughed, but it was more from embarrassment. "When I threatened Richard last night, that was the real me; the *me* that I've been trying to run away from for the last few years.

"I don't believe it."

Damien shrugged. "Well, whether or not you believe it, I did some pretty horrible things. The fact that I've kept my nose clean for the last couple years doesn't erase all of that."

"No, but it's a start."

"Obviously not enough of one, or I wouldn't be here."

Danni reached out and placed a hand on her knee. "It's not your fault that you're here. You don't deserve this."

He smiled at her. "Well, if it's any consolation, I think you should forgive yourself for your husband's death. Suicide was *his* choice. He could have just divorced you. Doing what he did was probably just his revenge. You should let it go."

She seemed like she might start sobbing at any moment, but somehow managed to smile back at him. "Thank you, Damien."

"You're welcome. Now come on, I fancy a drink."

"But I thought you didn't touch alcohol."

"I don't, but if I'm going to die, what the hell!"

He checked in the fridge and grabbed a beer. Danni asked for wine but there were no bottles left, so he headed over to the pantry. For a moment he worried that entering would seem like another attempt to escape, but when he tried the handle, it was locked. He banged the door with his fist and it held firm.

"They've cut us off," he said.

"That sucks," said Danni. "I wouldn't let Jade know or she'll kick off."

"And then she'll blame me," said Damien.

"No, I won't." Jade had heard his comment and was frowning at him from the sofa. "What would be the point in blaming you? *They* did this to us, not you. Still sucks, though. I could really do with a goddamn drink. I'm starting to stress about tomorrow when we have to start with their games all over again."

Damien took a swig of the beer and gasped at the harsh yet satisfying taste. "There's still plenty of beers left," he said. "We're not doomed just yet."

"HOUSEMATES, PLEASE ASSEMBLE IN THE LIVING AREA."

Jules leapt up from the sofa. "What? We're supposed to be safe tonight. They said no tasks."

"You goddamn LIARS," Jade shouted at the ceiling. "LIARS!"

Damien reached out to her. "Calm down, Jade. There's no point getting wound up."

Jade shoved him away. "Fuck you, Damien. Who do you think you are? Trying to tell everybody what to do like the Dalai Lama or something?"

Damien frowned at her. "What?"

"Just get the hell away from me." She stomped off towards the sofa.

Danni leant in and whispered. "She can flip like a switch, can't she?"

Damien decided not to take offence and went and sat on the sofa. He began to wonder what The Landlord had in store for them this time. He had said there would be no tasks, so what was going on?

"HOUSEMATES, TONIGHT THERE WILL BE A VOTE."

"What the hell?" said Jules. "No way."

"BUT THIS VOTE IS NOT FOR A TASK. TONIGHT THE HOUSEMATE WITH THE MOST VOTES WILL HAVE THEIR SINS REVEALED. YOU HAVE TEN MINUTES TO MAKE YOUR CHOICE."

"What does he mean by that?" asked Danni.

"Isn't it obvious?" Richard remarked snarkily. "Someone is going to get their video shown. Seeing as how you all have it in for me, I guess it's going to be mine."

"Not necessarily," said Damien. "We already know that you're an arsehole, so what would we have to gain from seeing your past transgressions?"

"Good point," said Danni. "Then who?"

"Maybe we shouldn't vote," said Patrick. The older man suddenly looked very nervous. "We can refuse."

Damien shook his head. "They'll just use the toxin on us, and believe me, you don't wanna feel that."

"Then what then?" Danni asked.

"How about spin the bottle?" Jules suggested. She was staring at one of the empty wine bottles on the table.

Everyone looked at one another and then Danni shrugged her shoulders. "Sounds good to me."

"Okay," said Damien. "Let's do it."

Everybody gathered in a circle around the table and then got down on their knees. Jade swiped an arm across the table to clear it of all debris. Then Jules placed the wine bottle in the centre of the table.

"Everybody ready?" she asked.

There were nervous nods all around. It seemed like nobody was happy about the prospect of having their 'sins' exposed, but they also all understood that there was no point fighting it.

Jules spun the wine bottle on the glass surface of the table. It spun fast, becoming a blurred circle.

Then it began to slow down, passing between those gathered around it.

Jade.

Damien.

Danni.

Tracey.

Richard.

Patrick.

Jules.

Jade.

Damien.

Danni.

Tracey.

Richard.

Patrick.

Jules.

Jade.

Damien...

Danni...

...Tracey...

...Richard...

...

...Patrick.

The bottle stopped on Patrick and immediately the older man's eyes went wide. He cleared his throat and stood up. He was trembling.

"Hey, Patrick," said Damien. "It's going to be okay."

"I...I don't want to see what they have on me. It will just be a whole load of lies. We don't even know that any of the videos we've seen are real. They could be manipulated. People can do anything with computers these days."

Damien nodded and smiled reassuringly. "I know. Don't worry. We all have secrets. We won't hold them against you."

"Depends what the secret is," said Richard.

Damien opened his mouth to object but then closed it again. Richard was right. Not everything was forgive-able.

"Oh God," said Patrick. "I feel quite sick. I think I'm going to get some fresh air in the garden."

Patrick left them all in the living room and headed out through the patio door. It had begun to rain again, but so far it was only a drizzle and a *pitter patter* at the window.

Behind them, on the television screen, a video began to play.

A handsome man in his twenties appeared alongside another man who might have been his twin. Both were wearing smart shirts and silky ties.

"In some ways we should thank Patrick Mitchell. If it wasn't for him, my brother and I would probably not have been driven to start up our successful chain of health spas. Our success came as a direct consequence of trying to run away from the people we were – the victims that we were made to be. But, as far as we've come and as hard as we've run, we've never been able to get away from that man. He's always with us – always will be.

The other brother took over. "Patrick Mitchell – *Mr*

Mitchell – was our third-year teacher when we were eight years old. He fucked us both. It didn't matter that we were children and that we cried out in pain, nothing would stop him sticking his dick in our mouths every chance he got. I doubt we were the only ones. He was good at frightening us into silence. Long enough that, by the time we had grown up enough to want to do something about it, we had already moved too far with our lives. We had become adults with families and children of our own. We couldn't put them through the hell of going public. Fortunately, having money allows you to do a lot of things in private. Paying for Patrick Mitchell's death is something we would do a hundred times over. I would gladly go bankrupt to see that man dead. I can't wait to see him suffer. I hope he thinks of us as he dies. I hope he sees our faces like we see his every night when we lie next to our wives."

The video finished. The word PREDATOR flashed on the screen.

18

"I'm going to bleedin' kill him," said Richard, leaping to his feet and grabbing the wine bottle up off the table. "That fucking nonce!"

"Just wait a minute," Damien said. "Don't do anything hasty."

Richard glared at Damien. "Are you kidding? The guy's a goddamn child molester. Nothing is worse."

Damien took a deep breath and held it. He didn't know what to do. He didn't condone violence – at least not anymore – but what Patrick had done made him feel sick to his soul. Despite wanting to do something to stop Richard, he found himself rooted to the spot as the furious man stormed out into the garden with the wine bottle grasped firmly in his hand.

"Hope he kills him," Jade said, sneering.

"We can't just start killing each other," said Jules.

"We can when it's a sick paedophile like Patrick."

"Maybe we should do something," Danni suggested to Damien.

Damien still didn't know what to do. He was conflicted.

He kept thinking of those poor brothers as children. What misery they must have gone through.

Outside, Patrick began to cry out.

That was enough to get Damien moving. He hurried out into the garden with the others following right behind him.

Richard was standing over Patrick in the rain by the wall with the eyeball painting. He had the bottle raised above his head. The bloody gash on Patrick's forehead suggested that he had already been struck at least once.

"Richard, wait," Damien yelled.

Richard spun around. "Why are you trying to stop me? This piece of shit needs putting down like a sick animal."

"I haven't done anything," Patrick whimpered on the ground. "Please leave me alone."

"You're a paedophile," Jade snarled at him. "You're an animal."

"I don't know what you're talking about. I was a good teacher. I never did anything wrong."

"Who said this had anything to do with you being a teacher?" said Damien.

Patrick shook his head. "W-what?"

"You said you were a good teacher, but we never said otherwise, which makes me think it's true that you abused your position."

Richard kicked Patrick in the ribs. "How many little boys did you bugger?"

Patrick howled in pain and scuttled along on his back like a crab. "Please," he begged. "It's all lies. I'm innocent. Please stop!"

Richard kicked him again. "Is that what the children used to say to you? Did you stop when they begged you to leave them alone?"

Suddenly Patrick's face twisted into one of fury. He spat

at Richard. "How dare you judge me. All of you are here for the same reason. You're all bad people – selfish people – evil people. You're all monsters. Yet you feel you have the right to judge me? I took what I wanted, just like all of you."

Damien shook his head. "Even evil has limits, Patrick. If you did what you've been accused of, then there's a special place in Hell for you."

"I'll see you all there," he spat.

Richard swung the bottle down again and it cracked off the side of Patrick's head. Patrick fell back onto the grass, cross-eyed and stunned. Richard knelt down and swung the bottle once more. The glass finally gave way and wicked shards showered the older man's face as the bottle smashed across his nose. He rolled onto his stomach and started crawling through the grass like a worm. Damien shook his head with pity.

Then he turned and walked away.

Richard stayed outside with the broken bottle and finished what he'd started, while the huge painted eye watched on.

DAY 6

"**H**OUSEMATES, PLEASE GATHER IN THE GARDEN FOR TODAY'S TASK."

Everybody got up from the sofa and headed out into the garden. Patrick lay dead at the far side of the courtyard. Nobody had bothered to move him. Sarah's body was a dozen feet past him, rotting in the corner of the courtyard. It was beginning to feel like a graveyard.

Today's task was earlier than usual. It still felt like morning to Damien, or at least early-afternoon. It was a cold, grey day and it looked like rain would resume at any moment.

The platform in the grass courtyard began to rise up out of the ground. This time it contained five glass containers full of clear liquid.

"THIS TASK IS MANDATORY. ALL HOUSEMATES MUST PARTICIPATE. IN FRONT OF YOU ARE FIVE SMALL VATS OF SULPHURIC ACID. HOUSEMATES ARE TO PLACE THEIR LEFT HANDS INTO EACH OF THE VATS. HOUSEMATE RICHARD MUST REMOVE THE BANDAGES PLACED ON HIS HAND FROM THE

PREVIOUS TASK. THE THREE HOUSEMATES THAT KEEP THEIR HAND IN THE ACID THE LONGEST WILL BE EXEMPT FROM TONIGHT'S TASK. THE OTHER TWO HOUSEMATES WILL GO HEAD TO HEAD."

Everybody groaned. "I can't do this," said Jules. "My hand is already messed up from ripping off all my nails."

"FAILURE TO ATTEMPT THE TASK WILL RESULT IN NEUROTOXIN BEING RELEASED."

Jules put her palms against her forehead and started to cry softly. She wasn't freaking out like she usually did and actually seemed resigned to having to do the task.

"This is really going to suck," said Tracey.

"Come on," said Jade. "Let's just get this over with."

Everyone lined up in front of the vats. The liquid was clear and odourless. Damien sighed as he looked at the innocuous substance. It looked no different to lemonade, but he knew it was far more deadly. A high school Chemistry lesson came back to him, making him remember something about sulphuric acid literally pulling the water from your skin cells and melting your flesh. It might have just been the teacher's way of scaring the class, but maybe it was true.

The anticipation of touching the liquid was enough to make Damien's stomach churn, but not participating would likely result in his death. As much as he had previously been ready to die, today was a new day and his will to survive had reasserted itself. The longer he stayed alive, the more chance he might have of an opportunity to fight back against his tormentors.

I managed to get at them once. Maybe I'll get another chance to finish the job.

They all waited while Richard removed the bandage

from his already injured hand. Then The Landlord got them started.

"HOUSEMATES, PUT YOUR HANDS INTO THE LIQUID IN 3...2...1..."

Everyone shoved their hands into the acid. For a couple of seconds there was silence as they no doubt expected to feel the caustic agony of the notorious chemical. But there was no pain at all, just a numb tingling sensation.

But that soon changed.

With growing ferocity, the slight tingling became a searing pain, like grasping a white-hot poker. The vats of clear liquid began to turn a mucky brown.

Damien bit at his lower lip as the pain kicked into sixth gear. He looked down at his hand and saw that it had gone an angry red. Wisps of smoke appeared and the liquid went murkier as his blood vessels broke apart and his flesh dissolved.

Jules screamed. Everybody else cursed and hissed. Damien bit harder into his lip and tasted blood.

Two seconds later, Jules could take no more and yanked her hand free. She collapsed to her knees and convulsed. Her screaming continued as she clutched her burnt appendage between her knees.

The other housemates continued to endure the agony. It grew worse every second.

Damien felt dizzy. The pain was like nothing he had ever felt. A deep, burning pinch that felt like a million red hot pins being pushed all the way down to the bone. The only thing that made him keep his hand in the acid was knowing that the other housemates were in just as much pain as he was. He just had to hold on a little longer, outlast one more person.

Tracey was the one to break next. The pain tolerance she

had showed in the previous tasks had not gotten her through this one. She pulled her hand out of the acid and screamed obscenities at the sky. As soon as she was away from the table, Richard, Danni, Jade, and Damien all yanked their own hands free of the acid. They cursed and snarled and they fought against the agony. The pain did not subside even though they had removed their hands from the bowls.

"HOUSEMATES TRACEY AND JULES WILL COMPETE IN TONIGHT'S HEAD TO HEAD."

"We need to go wash this stuff off," said Tracey, apparently uninterested in the proclamations of The Landlord that signalled her possibly ensuing death. She was a person that focused on the problems at hand, not the ones ahead.

"No," Damien shook his head. "I'm sure water will make it worse. It reacts."

"Screw that," said Richard. "I need cold water."

Everyone hurried inside and straight over to the kitchen. They shoved themselves into a huddle at the kitchen sink. To Damien's relief, the cold water didn't seem to be making anything worse. Richard sighed orgasmically as the cold water numbed his hand and seemed to gain relief from it.

"It's helping," Tracey informed Damien.

Damien nodded. "I'm glad I was wrong."

Everyone shoved their hands out in front of them and took turns getting their scorched flesh beneath the tap. Danni headed away from them, though.

"I'm going to the toilet," she said. "I can use the water there rather than fight with you all over a single tap."

Damien thought it was a good idea, although not exactly sanitary. He let her go.

Once he got his turn under the kitchen tap he gasped. The flesh of his hand was bright red and bubbling with the worst blisters he had ever seen. Blood seeped out of every pore and mixed with the water from the tap.

My whole hand is going to end up scarred.

If I live long enough to heal, that is.

Jade grabbed a beer from the fridge and downed it in a single, long gulp. Then she grabbed another one and started on it a little slower.

Damien turned around and opened the cupboard that housed the bandages they had got from the pantry after Richard's Bunsen burner task. He quickly got to work handing them out along with some antiseptic gauze in square packets.

He tore open his own packet with his teeth and laid the gauze on the back of his hand. It stung and reignited the pain. It didn't get any better as he wrapped the bandage around his hand and fastened it tightly.

Everybody helped one another get their wounds bandaged up before starting on what was left of the beers. Some hard liquor would have been better, but they had to take what they could find.

When Danni came out of the toilet she was clutching her injured hand under her armpit. Damien didn't see how the pain wasn't made worse by the friction, but didn't think about it too much. He handed her some gauze and asked if she needed any help getting her hand bandaged. She took the first aid supplies but declined his offer of help. Shrugging, Damien went to the fridge and grabbed himself one of the beers. It felt good to drink again. It made him feel more like the man he used to be. That man had been pretty repugnant, but he was also a tough son of a bitch. And being tough, right now, was exactly what he needed.

Whether it was the hormones brought on by the pain, or if something had merely snapped inside of Damien emotionally, he suddenly felt alive and ready. His senses were alert and all of the worries and concerns of his old life had been washed away as just one thing now became important: *survival*.

I'm Damien fucking Banks and I don't shit myself for no one.

Whatever you got for me next, Mr Landlord, bring it on.

You just better hope that it kills me.

19

"HOUSEMATES TRACEY AND JULES, please enter the Elimination Chamber."

Tracey wore a look of steely determination. Jules whimpered and fought with the rest of them as they were forced to grab a hold of her and shove her towards the door. She begged them not to make her go in the other room, but none of them listened. They had no choice. They hated sending her to a possible death, but it was either that or they all died for insubordination.

Damien felt like a hypocrite as he stood back and did nothing. He couldn't actively make himself force the poor girl inside the Elimination Chamber, but he wasn't doing anything to prevent it either. He just stood and watched as Richard, Danni, and Jade dragged the poor woman across the carpet.

Although I'm sure I wouldn't be as sympathetic if I saw her video. Funny how your view of someone can be so wrong. If anything, the videos I have seen have opened my eyes to some things.

I wonder what my video will show.

Damien wished some wonderful plan would come to him – a tarnished gem of an idea that slowly became a clear-cut diamond of inspiration – but nothing entered his mind. As much as he wanted to do something for Jules, there was no course of action that made any sense to him.

So he stood by and did nothing as Tracey and Jules were shoved inside what would no doubt become their torture chamber. Their only hope was to be the victor in whatever task was presented to them. That was what had gotten Damien through the two occasions he had entered that room.

The television screen lit up with the live feed and everybody sat down to watch. Today the white cube room was occupied by what looked like a pair of old-fashioned pommel horses, except the wooden body of the structure was pointed like a pyramid – an oak wedge on sturdy legs. On both sides of the wedge was what looked like stirrups. They were attached to the ground by steel cables.

"HOUSEMATES TRACEY AND JULES, PLEASE STEP UP ONTO THE APPARATUS IN FRONT OF YOU BY PLACING YOUR FEET INSIDE THE STIRRUPS."

Tracey and Jules both stood there for a moment, stiff like boards. Tracey was the first to take the step forward, probably hoping that enthusiasm would be the thing to get her through. She climbed up onto the wooden horse and secured both bare feet inside the stirrups.

Then, visibly shaking, Jules did the same. She was weeping as she climbed up and secured herself in place.

Danni was sat next to Damien on the sofa. She leant in and asked him, "What are those things? They look like a pair of badly made rocking horses."

Damien shook his head. "I don't know what they are, but I'm starting to get an idea of what they're intended for."

"HOUSEMATES TRACEY AND JULES, PLEASE STAND BY. THE TASK IS ABOUT TO BEGIN."

There was a loud *clank* as the metal stirrups clamped around the two women's ankles. Both of them yelped in surprise and perhaps pain, depending on how tight the ankle cuffs were.

"THE APPARATUS ON WHICH YOU SIT IS CALLED A SPANISH DONKEY. IT IS A DEVICE DATING BACK TO TIMES OF THE INQUISITION. ITS INTENTION WAS TO EXTRACT CONFESSIONS. THAT IS ITS PURPOSE TODAY."

There was a short silence while the Landlord's words seemed to hang in the air. Then he continued.

"EACH OF YOU IS HERE FOR A REASON. EACH OF YOU KNOW THE SECRET THAT CONDEMNS YOU. YOU HAVE SPENT YOUR LIVES TRYING TO HIDE YOUR ONE BIG SIN, BUT THERE ARE NO SECRETS IN THIS HOUSE. YOUR PAST HAS BEEN PLACED UPON THE SCALES OF JUSTICE AND BEEN FOUND WANTING. REVEAL YOUR BIGGEST SIN...OR DIE."

Silence filled the house, both inside and outside of the Elimination chamber. Nothing seemed to be happening and Tracey and Jules shifted uncomfortably on their wooden perches.

Then there was an almighty grinding of unseen gears and the two ladies cried out in pain.

"What's happening?" Danni asked. Her brow was wrinkled and it was clear that she did not understand what was going on. The view on the television screen showed no obvious cause for the women's pain, but there was indeed a subtle difference, and Damien noticed it.

"The steel chains have gone taut. The stirrups are being pulled towards the floor."

Danni looked at him for a moment and then at the television screen. She seemed to finally understand. "My God!" she said, cupping her bandaged hand to her mouth.

Inside the elimination Chamber, there was another sound of grinding gears.

Tracey and Jules bellowed in pain. Their bodies were being pulled down onto the wooden wedge and the pressure was threatening to split them apart from the groin as their legs were yanked down on either side. Both women thrashed and fumbled at their wooden perches, trying to scramble away, but their ankles held them in place.

There was another grinding of gears.

Jules begged for mercy; so did Tracey.

The gears turned again.

Jules threw up on herself and wobbled wearily on the horse. The pain was threatening to tug her into unconsciousness.

Tracey shook her head and gritted her teeth. It seemed like she was trying with all her might not to cry out. Perhaps she was trying to prevent herself from confessing whatever it was that The Landlord demanded she admit to.

Another grinding of gears and the women's legs looked like they might pop apart at the knees. Their entire bodies were stretched taught and the wedge seemed to drive up several inches into their vaginas.

"It's going to split them in half," said Danni.

Another grinding of gears and the ankle restraints tightened yet again. The shackles were now several inches closer to the ground than when the task had started.

Jules seemed to collapse in place, her shoulders and head slumping sideways but her lower body unable to move. Despite her physical breakdown, she began to mutter something. The speakers in the ceiling amplified so that everyone could hear her words.

"I...I...slept with my sister's husband. Then...one night... I found her in...the bathtub. She had...cut herself...."

Damien tilted his head and listened intently. The story sounded oddly familiar.

Jules seemed to lose consciousness for a moment, but then lifted her head and carried on.

"I...I...wanted her husband and to have...to have our business...our salon...all to myself. I left her there to die. I didn't call an ambulance. I just went...home. But her husband...he didn't want me...he blamed me...he closed the salon. He left me with...nothing."

"HOUSEMATE JULES, YOU HAVE CONFESSED YOUR BIGGEST SIN. CONGRATULATIONS."

The ankle restraints around Jule's ankles sprung open. She slumped sideways and fell awkwardly to the floor. There she lay, panting and moaning."

"HOUSEMATE TRACEY. YOU HAVE NOT CONFESSED YOUR SINS, THEREFORE YOU WILL DIE."

Tracey was visibly weak from the pain, but her voice was strong as she shouted up at the ceiling. "No, please. I'll confess. I'll tell you the-"

The gears cranked.

Then they cranked again.

Tracey howled in agony. Blood began to leak down her legs and drip from the tips of her toes.

The gears cranked again.

And again.

And again.

Tracey's eyes began to roll into the back of her head. Her body was now pulled so tightly against the wooden pyramid that it seemed like a part of her body.

The gears cranked again.

Tracey's head slumped forward. She was either dead or unconscious.

The gears continued turning.

Clank! Clank! Clank!

Tracey's body began to split. Her legs pulled apart like the wishbone from a turkey. Her body lost its form, no long even resembling the shape of a human.

The gears finally stopped turning.

"HOUSEMATES, PLEASE ENTER THE ELIMINA-TION CHAMBER AND REMOVE HOUSEMATE JULES. THE PANTRY HAS BEEN RESTOCKED WITH SUPPLIES. ENJOY."

20

F ive housemates left and Jules in such a state that she might not even make it through the night.

They had dragged her out of the Elimination Chamber and onto the sofa. She was bleeding from between her legs, but it wasn't arterial. Her internal workings had been badly damaged, but luckily it seemed like nothing had ruptured. Tracey on the other hand had looked like she'd exploded. Blood pooled beneath her body as if every organ in her body had torn open. The smell of faeces and urine had also been present. The housemates had been sure to avoid her as they dragged out Jules.

Now everybody was sitting on the sofa, drinking the restocked supplies of alcohol and staring into space. They were all obviously thinking about their own survival and how impossible it seemed, but also perhaps about their existence and how they had spent it. Damien was certainly assessing a few things in his own mind.

He thought about his friend, Harry. Harry would have told him not to lose hope, that God would protect those who deserved protecting.

But if I'm in this house, doesn't that mean that I'm beyond salvation? Isn't this house full of deplorable sinners? If I'm here then I must be one, too. The fact that I don't know what I've done must mean that I'm the worst of all. I don't even see the consequences of my own actions. I am unrepentant.

Damien rubbed at his face and felt the fuzzy tiredness in his eyes. The longer this all went on, the more and more he needed sleep. With a bedroom containing Catherine's corpse and the sofa not designed for napping on, it was difficult to snooze long and deep. The exhaustion was beginning to take its toll. But as much as Damien felt tired, he still also felt strong and fearless. He knew that with the right opportunity, he would still have what it took to strike. His only intention now, since survival seemed impossible, was to enact revenge on at least one of the monsters that kept him here. For they were monsters, too.

The television screen came on. It displayed the word WHORE. An audio tape recording of a man's voice began to play.

"Tracey was one of the best politicians I know. She fought for equality, human rights, and safety within our society. I don't know why she eventually quit at such a young age, but then a lot of things in politics cannot always be explained. I had heard rumours that she was planning to move abroad with the small fortune she had inherited from her mother.

My respect ran much deeper than mere attraction for her. I was sad when she decided that she no longer wished to date me, but there wasn't much I could do, so I said goodbye and tried to move on.

A few months later, when I began feeling under the weather – I was constantly getting the sniffles and stomach aches – I went to see my doctor in Hammersmith. He had a pretty grotty office, but he was good at what he did and I had always been a happy patient of his. Still, when he told me that my blood test results came back HIV positive, I doubted him. I thought maybe the old guy had lost it. But when my results came back the second time, from a different physician, I had no choice but to accept what I had been told."

The tape crackled for a moment, but then cleared up.

"The thing that I couldn't get my head around was that the only person I had slept with in the last year or so was Tracey. I couldn't fathom that it may have been her that had given it to me. She must not have known. I was furious at her, but also saddened and sympathetic as a fellow sufferer of a terrible disease that we both now shared. I thought I would be delivering devastating news to her, but when I told her, she didn't seem worried at all. A couple weeks later, she gave me a call to say that her own results had come back negative. I didn't understand how that was possible. The stupid fool that I was, I even apologised to her for causing her undue stress and worry. She told me not to worry about it but to tell no one that we had slept together as it could damage her reputation. Of course I promised to keep my mouth shut."

The tape crackled again, this time for longer.

"It wasn't until James Jeffrey stepped down from the cabinet, due to undisclosed health reasons, that I became suspicious. I mixed in the same circles as James and I also knew that he was a friend of Tracey's. I went and visited him at home. After some gentle prodding, he admitted that he had HIV and that he had also given it to his wife. He admitted to cheating on her frequently and was now paying the price. When I asked for some names, he reluctantly gave them to me. Tracey was among the list of women."

After some digging – not all of it legal – I managed to

discover that Tracey had been diagnosed with the disease two years before I even slept with her. She had HIV and was spreading it around without any shred of a conscience. She had given it to me in the throes of passion that, at the time, I assumed were the beginnings of real love and affection. I had been upset when she had ended it, but what I felt at that moment went far beyond mere anger. I wanted the woman dead. After all, she had killed me, one way or the other. I thought about going to the Police, but I knew that it would destroy the reputations of any fellow politician that had been involved with her. Many were innocent like me. I decided to deal with things unofficially. I once heard about an organisation that could solve these kinds of problems. Luckily a friend of mine had their contact information – he had used them to take care of a man who had assaulted his wife. I paid their asking price happily. I might die one day due to this disease, but at least I will go knowing that Tracey died first. Revenge is one of the few pleasures left to me."

The tape crackled and ended.

The television changed from displaying the word WHORE to the grid of twelve silhouettes. Beneath the photo of Jules was the word, CHEAT. Beneath the photo of Tracey was the word WHORE. The remaining silhouettes were attached to the words PEDDLER, CRUSADER, MURDERER, and TRAITOR.

DAY 7

Damien was sat alone in the living area, cracking his knuckles as he put some of his mental ducks in a row. Everybody else, surprisingly, was enjoying the hot tub in the garden, smoking fags and a new supply of alcohol from the newly reinforced pantry. Although the bubbling water was grimy, the trace amount of chlorine was still the best way available to get clean inside the house. Damien himself would probably join them a little later.

The bracelet on his wrist had been taunting him for the last hour while he sat alone. The blinking LED lights seemed to be winking at him. The fact that something clung to his body and would not remove itself was frustrating on a very basic level – like finding a tick on your body and crushing it in anger.

It was still hard to believe the situation he was in. Only a few weeks ago life had been normal, even a little mundane. Damien had spent his days carving wood and fixing joints. He leased a modest flat and wasted his nights shooting *noobs* on Xbox Live. As much as Damien had turned his life around over the last few years, he realised now that there was still room for improvement. He could have been living life more than he had been. Now he wouldn't get the chance.

The main reason Damien had been drawn to crime as a teenager, besides being surrounded by it, was his father. The great Jan Olsson, son of Swedish immigrants, made a name for himself in the suburbs of Birmingham – Redditch, Bromsgrove, Studley, and Alcester mostly. Drugs, prostitution, violence for hire, he had his fingers in a lot of crud-filled pies. But robbing banks had been too much of a stretch for Damien's kingpin of a father. The bungling idiot had been caught and arrested on his very first try; a shoddy attempt to rob an Evesham building society. He got fifteen years.

But Damien had still been under his father's influence, even with him banged up. He was expected to keep 'the firm' running in his old man's absence. Damien had done his best for a while – intimidating people and selling his father's drugs – but it wasn't who he was.

But he had no way out. His father's influence was everywhere. Damien had been forced to commit to the role and had done many things he regretted.

Which is the reason I am here.

But then Harry had come along. At first Damien thought nothing of the man who had started drinking himself to death in the local pub. Harry was just another drunk.

But then one day, the man just stopped drinking cold turkey; never touched a drop again. It was like he had woken up one morning a changed man. When Damien found out that the man's heavy drinking was all because of losing his young son to a drunk driver, Damien's opinion of the man had softened. The man's love for his son, even years after his death, was honourable.

For some reason Harry saw something in Damien, too, and reached out with a job offer. Even more fortuitous, he presented an opportunity to move away and leave their old lives behind. They both needed to start again – to leave the painful past behind them.

Together the two of them moved north and started a business and a new existence. Damien had quickly come to view Harry as somewhat of a replacement father. Harry was kind hearted and intelligent, with a knack for seeing the best in people. He had helped Damien become a better man.

I'll never thank him enough for that.

But then Harry had got sick.

It began with vomiting and headaches.

Then he went partially blind in one eye.

By the time Harry went to see a specialist, the brain tumour was the size of a golf ball. *Glioblastoma multiforme* – one of the worst kinds of cancer. Harry had less than two years.

That was why Damien was in this abominable house – the sole fucking reason. The World Health Organisation was running clinical trials for *boron neutron capture therapy.* It was experimental, but had begun to show promising results. It was perhaps the only chance Harry had, but it cost three-hundred thousand pounds. Add on the cost of getting to South Africa and living there for up to twelve months while the treatment was underway and it became a hopeless dream. Which was why Damien had allowed himself to be convinced by the stranger who had visited him with the proposition of winning the money he needed. Take part in a reality television show for the chance to win up to two million pounds. It must have been fate. Harry would have said that God was offering him a chance, but the truth was that it was Damien who was being offered the chance and he had to take it.

Harry had agreed to him going, so long as he "kept his integrity." He said that Damien had worked so hard to become successful and respectful that he couldn't let a bunch of television producers bring him down.

But it had all been a set-up. Damien had made a deadly mistake. That mistake left Harry with no hope of survival and, even worse, now no one would even be there by his side at the end. The thought filled Damien with anger. He clenched his fists and snorted.

"You okay?" Danni was heading through the patio doors from the garden and shivering. She was wearing a bikini that Jade had lent to her. She looked at him and frowned.

"I'm fine," he said. "Just...reflecting."

She took a seat next to him and brought her knees up on the sofa. The soles of her feet were covered in blades of grass. "I've been doing that, too," she said. "I don't know how I haven't gone crazy yet. I mean, we're all going to die. Why are we not panicking?"

Damien chewed the inside of his cheek and wondered about the answer. "I suppose we've all realised that panicking isn't going to help, so why waste the energy? If these are our last days then there are more productive things to do than scream."

"But we're all just sitting here and accepting it. We're like lambs lined up in a slaughterhouse."

Damien shrugged. "What can we do different."

"You tell me. You're the one that told us to be ready for an opportunity."

"And an opportunity is yet to present itself. Don't worry, though, I'm ready."

"Good," she said, lying up against him, "because I'm relying on you to save us all."

Damien chuckled. "No pressure then?"

"Hey, I'm just asking you to give it a shot. What do you have to lose?"

"Nothing, I guess."

Damien suddenly had a thought. It was something that had been bothering him since last night. "You told me that you were the *whore.*"

Danni flinched slightly at the word and then looked at him in confusion. "What?"

"When I asked you what word on the television belonged to you, you told me that it was *whore.* You told me about how you cheated on your husband and how he killed himself."

Danni nodded. Her eyes wandered off to the side as she failed to look at him. "That's right. He killed himself because of what I did. I don't want to go over it all again. It's painful."

Damien nodded at her. He rubbed one of his hands down her naked arm. "Sorry."

"It's okay."

"It's just that one thing confuses me," said Damien.

"What?"

"Tracey was the one identified as being the *whore.* Plus Jules's confession in the task that beat Tracey sounded a lot like the story you told me."

Danni eyes narrowed at him and she seemed to be getting annoyed. "So?"

"Well, don't you think it's strange?"

Danni looked angry for a few moments, but then her face softened. She let out a long sigh and rubbed a hand against her forehead. "I lied," she admitted. "Jules told me why she thought she was in here and I copied her story when you asked me what my sins were."

"That makes no sense," said Damien. "If she so happily confessed her secrets to you, then why did she resist during the task? She was almost ripped apart by the time she admitted to what she had done."

Danni shrugged. "I don't know. She was drunk and confiding in me. I told her some secrets too. Maybe that's why she trusted me."

"So what is the real reason you are here?"

"Honestly...I don't know. I'm not supposed to be here."

Damien rolled his eyes. "Welcome to the club."

Danni shook her head. "No, I mean I'm really not supposed to be here. The people in charge here wanted Danielle Robinson but my name is Danielle Anderson. I'm Danielle Robinson's PA."

"I don't understand," said Damien.

"When my boss was visited by a strange man and given the opportunity to enter the house and win the prize money she said she wasn't interested. The stranger seemed disappointed. He left a card with an email address and told Danielle to contact him if she changed her mind. She didn't. So I made a rash decision."

"You pretended to be her?"

Danni nodded. "We look alike. Same figure, same hair, same age. Only difference was that she was successful and I was fetching her overpriced cups of coffee. I thought that if I pretended to be her I could change my life. Even if the show producers found out, I would already have gotten my face on television. It could be enough to change my life.

"Guess that's exactly what it did."

Danni laughed. "No shit! Looks like my sins are catching up with me whether I'm supposed to be here or not."

Damien shook his head and thought about it. As much as he felt like a victim for being in the situation he was, Danni was even more so. She hadn't even done anything wrong to warrant being in the house.

"That really sucks," he said.

"Yep, really does. Still, not much I can do about it now." She moved closer to him, close enough that her shivering, almost-naked body was right up against his. Her face was only inches away from his own.

"What are you doing?" he asked her.

"I don't want to be a lamb in the slaughterhouse anymore. I'm not dead yet."

She kissed Damien on the mouth. He resisted for a moment, but then wondered why and allowed himself to go with it. He kissed her back and she draped her naked leg over him and got even closer. Damien felt himself growing hard as his hands roved the smooth skin of her thigh.

Danni felt the erection and stopped kissing him. She smiled and purred. "Who's a big boy then?"

Damien blushed.

"Get a room or I'll spray you both with the hose!"

The other housemates had all re-entered the living area and were standing in a shivering huddle. Jules was grinning and giggling like a schoolgirl, despite the obvious pain that caused her to hunch over like an old woman. It was ironic to see her appreciate their affection after yesterday admitting how she had coldheartedly watched her sister die.

Damien eased Danni away from him and composed himself. He was forced to place both hands over his lap.

"Good to see you have your priorities straight," said

Richard. "Maybe you should be thinking more about how to get out of here and less about your todger."

Damien shrugged. "And I suppose you have a ton of ideas?"

"We're expecting The Landlord," said Jules, easing down very gingerly onto the sofa. It appeared she might recover from her injuries, but it would take some time. Probably time she would never have. "It's getting dark," she said, "and we haven't been given a task yet."

Jade sighed. "More fun and games. Can't wait."

Damien felt his erection dissipate and was comfortable enough to get up from the sofa. He glanced outside the patio windows and saw that the light outside was growing grey. All of the other tasks they had done had been during daylight hours, followed by a head to head elimination in the evening.

"Well, I'm going to go put some clothes on before I freeze," said Danni, slithering up off the sofa and brushing past Damien teasingly.

Richard whistled at Damien once she was out of earshot. "Looks like you decided to go out with a bang, if you know what I mean."

Damien nodded. "You're a master of the single entendre, Richard."

Richard frowned. "So, what's the plan? What do we do if we get another task?"

"We don't have much choice but to do it. The Landlord will release the toxin if we don't."

"Well, maybe that's for the best," said Jade. "We could end all this now. We just refuse to cooperate."

Jules looked at Jade with her mouth open. "And just let The Landlord kill us?"

"We're dead anyway. At least this way would be on *our* terms."

"I agree," said Damien. "If I can't get at the people doing this, then the least I can do is end their sadistic little games. Never thought I would ever contemplate suicide but...if we're going to die anyway?"

"Then we're going to do this, then?" asked Richard incredulously. "We're just going to give up?"

"Giving up would be carrying on like rats in a maze," said Damien. "This is the only way we can actually go out on our own terms. It's the only way *not* to give up."

Richard stared down at the floor but nodded his head. "Okay, then. I'm in. Maybe if I'm lucky my corpse will shit itself when they try and carry me out of here."

Everybody agreed to abstain from any tasks. When Danni came back to the living area in a change of clothes, they brought her up to speed.

"So, we just...do nothing?"

Damien nodded. "It's either that or we just go through another few days of pain and suffering and then die anyway. We want to just end this now."

"But the Landlord said that they will still honour the winner. They said that the prize money was still up for grabs."

"You don't really believe that, do you?" asked Jade. "There's no way they can let any of us out of here alive."

"Why not," Danni said. "We don't know who any of them are, or even where they're keeping us? They could just blindfold us and dump us somewhere and we'd be none the wiser."

"This won't work without all of us onboard," said Jade. "I know it's crazy how calmly we're all discussing it, but when the alternative is torture and eventual death, the idea becomes easier."

Danni shook her head. "I...I just don't know if I can do it. I...I'll see how I feel when the task is announced. I think we should all see what we're up against before we make any decisions."

Damien scratched at his chin and realised that he had the fuzz of a half-grown beard. "Okay," he said. "We'll play things by ear."

"HOUSEMATES, PLEASE GATHER IN THE GARDEN. YOUR TASK IS ABOUT TO BEGIN."

Damien started towards the patio door. "Guess it's time to find out what we're made of."

21

As always, the platform in the garden began to rise up from the surrounding grass, right in front of the painting of an eye. Today it featured a large, multi-coloured wheel. It didn't matter what it was for, because Damien, and hopefully the other housemates, were not going to play along.

The large wheel locked into place. It was about seven feet high and cast a long shadow beneath a spotlight affixed to the back of it. At the top of the wheel was an arrow, cut roughly from a scrap of metal. The wheel itself was divided into five segments. Each segment had the name and face of a housemate.

"HOUSEMATES, BEFORE YOU IS A WHEEL OF FORTUNE LIKE NO OTHER. IT WILL DECIDE YOUR FATE."

Damien rolled his eyes. *That's what you think. You can take that wheel and roll it right up your arse.*

"ONE HOUSEMATE MUST COME FORWARD AND SPIN THE WHEEL. WHOEVER IT LANDS ON WILL BE

SELECTED FOR TONIGHT'S SOLO ELIMINATION TASK."

"What's a solo elimination task?" Jules asked.

Damien shrugged. "Who cares? We're not playing along, remember?"

Jules nodded. She seemed anxious, but even more weak and weary. However afraid she might be, it was obvious that she had had enough. She was ready for it all to end. Jules, perhaps more than anyone, had felt the tortures of this house in full force.

"WILL ONE OF THE HOUSEMATES PLEASE NOW SPIN THE WHEEL."

Instead, all of the housemates sat down on the grass. Damien propped his elbows up on his knees and rested his head in his hands. He relaxed his breathing and prepared himself for the pain that the toxin would soon bring.

"HOUSEMATES, PLEASE COMPLY."

"How about you bite me?" said Jade.

"Yeah," Richard growled. "Why don't you go back to the puddle of shit you climbed out of?"

"HOUSEMATES, REFUSAL TO CO-OPERATE WILL RESULT IN EXPULSION FROM THE HOUSE."

"Big whoop!" said Jules. "We've had enough of your crap."

Damien looked at Jules, smiled and nodded. Then he looked up at the starry night sky and smiled even wider. At least they couldn't take the view away.

"You're just going to have to kill us," said Damien. "We're through taking orders."

"SO BE IT."

The pain started immediately. Ice and fire combined in every sinew of muscle, blood turning to broken glass in their veins.

Everyone tumbled onto their sides and scrunched up into the foetal position. It did not help a great deal, but there was some comfort in going out the same way you came in. Jules threw up in the grass. The brownish goop covered her chin as she moaned.

Richard pulled so hard at his bracelets that blood began to flow down his wrists as flesh was shorn away by the sharp edges of metal. Mostly, though, they all fought the pain bravely. Each of them fought off the urge to scream in favour of a muffled growl of anguish. Danni hissed and rocked back and forth in the grass. Tears flooded down her cheeks. Damien tried to move over to her, but his muscles cramped and made the short crawl impossible.

"SPIN THE WHEEL, MAKE IT STOP."

Damien felt a pinch in his neck, followed by a slight alleviation of pain. He was still in agony, but his muscles had unlocked and stopped their cramping. The Landlord was giving them all a taster of the relief available from the counter-agent.

"THIS IS YOUR FINAL WARNING. SPIN THE WHEEL OR ALL OF YOU WILL DIE."

"Screw you!" Damien spat.

"Yeah," said Richard. "Bring it on. I love this shit."

Everyone remained on the ground, in pain and waiting for more. They all remained resolute that this was how they wanted to go out, in a feat of courage and endurance – maybe even bravery. Perhaps for some of them it was a means of redemption, a baptism of fire.

Danni wobbled up onto her knees. She clutched at the grass in front of her and let out an animalistic moan.

"Just lie down," Damien told her. "It will all be over in a minute."

"I don't want it to be over," she said. "I don't want to die."

She began crawling on her hands and knees towards the wheel. She dug her fingers into the grass as she went, as if doing so would help propel her onwards.

"Don't do it," said Damien. "It will only result in more pain. We can end this now."

"Get back here, bitch," Richard said.

Danni shook her head and kept crawling forward. In normal circumstances, Damien could have caught up to her in a single stride but, overloaded with so much pain, he was forced to watch her make it over to the wheel.

When she got there, Danni used the scaffolds that held the wheel in place to pull herself back to her feet. Her legs were wobbly like a new born fowl, but she managed to stay upright. She placed both hands on the wheel and then let her full weight fall upon it. She collapsed to the ground, but not before giving the wheel a great big yank on the way down.

The wheel spun.

The faces and names of the housemates became a whirl as they chased each other in a circle. Each revolution of the wheel resulted in a *click click click*. It really was just like a game show.

The most twisted, messed-up game show of all time.

Damien watched in horror as the wheel began to slow down. The other housemates, including Danni, just lay on the grass and watched with wide eyes.

Click click click!

The wheel got slower and slower.

Click...click...click!

...click!

...

...

Click!

"HOUSEMATE DAMIEN WILL PERFORM TONIGHT'S SOLO ELIMINATION."

Damien felt the counter-agent flood in through his collar. He sighed, not with relief, but with defeat. The torment was not yet over. Danni had condemned him to another task.

She lay several feet away, tears streaming down her face as she looked at him. She shook her head over and over and mouthed the words, "I'm sorry."

But apologies weren't going to help anyone.

22

Danni had been apologising to Damien incessantly since the incident in the garden. He had already accepted her apology, saw no reason not to as it changed very little. He would just refuse the elimination task and do what he intended to do earlier. If Danni still held on to hope for survival then good for her. He would not begrudge her that.

Jade on the other hand was less forgiving.

"You bitch," she shouted at Danni. "We all just went through a shitload of agony for no reason."

"I'm sorry. I'm so sorry. I just don't want to die."

Jade shoved Danni hard, sending her stumbling back on her bare feet. "We's gonna die anyhow. You just made damn sure it's gonna hurt worse."

Danni started crying. "Jade, I'm sorry. I didn't mean to do what I did. I just couldn't help it."

Jade went to shove Danni again, but Damien stepped between the two women. "Come on. It doesn't matter now. What's done is done."

"Like hell it is," said Jade. "I'm going to fuck her up for what she just did."

Danni whimpered.

Damien shot Jade a look that he hoped showed that he meant business. "Nobody is doing anything. We are going to sit down, have a drink, and wait for my task to begin. Anything else is just a waste of energy best spent elsewhere."

Jade met his stare and seemed in no way threatened, but eventually she relented and took a step back. "Fine, but just so you know. I don't trust that bitch. She's been fanning around this place since the beginning like it's a goddamn vacation. Why is it that everyone gets how serious this is but her?"

"I do understand the situation we're in," Danni said. "I just haven't given up yet."

"Cus you haven't felt no pain yet. At least, not like the rest of us. I swear, next chance I get I'm sending you into that white room."

"Enough with the threats, Jade," said Damien. "Correct me if I'm wrong but you haven't been in an elimination task either."

Jade held up her left hand covered in a thick bandage. "There's a reason for that!"

"We've all done what we've had to to stay alive, so why blame Danni for doing the same?"

Jade rolled her eyes and gave up the argument. "I'm just saying that I don't trust her. She ain't like the rest of us."

I know, Damien thought. *She's the only one here who is actually innocent.*

"HOUSEMATE DAMIEN, PLEASE ENTER THE ELIMINATION CHAMBER."

"What are you going to do?" Richard asked him.

Damien sighed. I'm going to go inside, see what the score is. Likelihood is that I'll refuse the task. That might mean the rest of you getting a dose from the bracelets. You good with that?"

Richard nodded. "Do what you have to do. Nothing's changed from earlier. I'm still tired of this shit."

Damien nodded and turned away. He marched over to the elimination chamber's door and felt a growing numbness. Even the fear of pain, and the agony itself, was becoming tolerable. For the most part he was already dead.

He opened up the door and stepped inside the white cube room. This time in the centre was a small table with a glass box on it. From over by the door, it was unclear what was inside the box.

"HOUSEMATE DAMIEN, YOU WISH TO DIE SO HERE IS YOUR OPPORTUNITY. IN THE CENTRE OF THE ROOM IS A BOX. INSIDE THE BOX IS THE TOOL YOU NEED TO END YOUR LIFE. PLEASE PICK IT UP."

Not yet following, Damien went over to the glass box and opened it up. He found an ornate looking revolver inside of it. It was heavy in his hand.

"IN YOUR HAND IS A WEBLEY MK. IV REVOLVER. IT TOOK THE LIFE OF GERMANS IN BOTH WORLD WARS. NOW IT MIGHT TAKE YOURS. A SINGLE BULLET SITS WITHIN ITS SIX CYLINDERS. YOU MUST FIRE THE REVOLVER AT YOUR SKULL ONCE AND THEN AT THE CEILING ONCE. REPEAT THIS UNTIL YOU ARE EITHER DEAD OR YOU HAVE FIRED THE BULLET AT THE CEILING. IF YOU ARE STILL ALIVE AT THE END OF THE TASK, YOUR RIGHT BRACELET WILL BE REMOVED."

Damien's eyes went wide. Did he just hear right? If he survived this sick game of Russian roulette then he would be half way to escaping the neurotoxin clamped around his wrists.

Are they seriously considering letting a winner go at the end of all this? Or is it just a sick game to make us all think there's a way out.

Damien felt sure that the gesture was just a ploy designed to prevent a revolt like the one that happened earlier in the garden. Still, it was a means to an end. If Damien got one of the bracelets off then he only had one more to worry about.

Damien nodded and raised the pistol up against the side of his head. He closed his eyes and had to stop himself from chuckling. Of all the times he had seen this kind of thing in the movies, he never once imagined that it would happen to him.

Well, it'll be a story to tell the grandkids if I ever get out of this hellhole.

Damien took a deep breath and placed his forefinger against the trigger. Slowly he applied pressure.

Click!

A great gust of relief burst forth from Damien's lungs and he actually laughed, somewhat maniacally.

He pointed the revolver at the ceiling and pulled the trigger again.

Click!

Damn it. Two down, one in four chance left.

He placed the revolver's muzzle back against his temple and took in another deep breath and held it. He squeezed the trigger again.

Paused for a moment.

And then...*Click!*

Jesus goddamn bleeding Christ.

He let out another sigh of relief.

He pointed the revolver back at the ceiling and pulled the trigger.

Click!

Oh God no. Fifty-fifty chance left. Heads I live, tails I die.

Damien took a few, increasingly anxious breaths and felt his heart beating right up against his ribs. His lungs no longer obeyed him and pumped erratically on their own.

Slowly, he lowered the revolver back to his head. He nudged the muzzle against his temple. If this bullet was going to kill him, he wanted to make sure it went straight through his brain; none of that lodged in the right/left hemisphere and paralyzed for life palaver. If this was it, he wanted to do it clean. He pressed the revolver harder against his skull, causing stars to invade his vision.

Here goes. My dad always said there was honour in dying by a bullet.

Fuck him!

Damien pulled the trigger.

Click!

"Jesus effing Christ," he said out loud. A huge smile had taken control of his face and he was gushing as excited breaths spilled forth from his lungs.

He quickly pointed the revolver at the ceiling and pulled the trigger one last time.

Bang!

The explosion of the bullet leaving the chamber made Damien cry out in fright, but he was soon back to laughing as ceiling plaster rained down on him like snow.

"Woo! That shit was intense. I'm alive, baby!"

Damien felt positively insane and he had to mentally take note to take control of himself. He forced his breathing to slow down and tried to calm down. The urge to take a piss became urgently strong. Even after resigning himself to death, the act of avoiding the grim reaper through a game of chance had reignited a fuse inside of him that he thought had gone out.

The bracelet on Damien's right wrist suddenly sprung open and hit the floor with a *clank*. The relief was instant and he immediately started rubbing at the irritated flesh that had been held captive for so many days. Suddenly it felt like freedom was a tangible pursuit, and not just the hopeless dream it had seemed earlier in the day.

Damien was still feeling a little manic, but he was calming down gradually as he began to have several thoughts; amongst them was one clear intention.

I'm going to get out of this goddamn house alive.

"CONGRATULATIONS, HOUSEMATE DAMIEN. PLEASE LEAVE THE ELIMINATION CHAMBER."

Damien did as he was told.

DAY 8

Damien hadn't realised the weight of the bracelets until one of them was gone. As he lay now on the sofa, staring out at the dew-soaked grass of the garden, he couldn't help but rub at his liberated wrist over and over again.

Last night he had actually managed to get a little sleep. From the snoring going on around him, so did everybody else. With one of Damien's bracelets gone, they had all opened up to the possibility that they might get out of there. There was a chance that the winner would be set free – and maybe the runner up as well.

If The Landlord actually kept his word and honoured the contest, then it made everything a muddled mystery again. If all the housemates were there to die, then it was easy to believe that this was all just a revenge for hire scheme that people had paid into. But if anybody was allowed to walk out of here alive then things were obviously more complex than that. What about the person that had paid for revenge? Would they accept their candidate walking free? If there was a winner at the end of all this, then was it really a game show? And if so, then who the hell was watching?

Now that he had stirred from slumber, there was no way that Damien could fall back to sleep, so he got up from the sofa and went over to the kitchen. The last resupply had provided them with some fresh coffee and tea as well as the usual ample amounts of alcohol. Damien thumbed the switch for the kettle and took a seat on the stool as he waited for the water inside to boil.

Back home, he would often stick the kettle on for Harry, who was an avid tea drinker. Damien preferred coffee. In light of what had happened concerning his bracelets, he wondered if there was still the opportunity to win the prize money. If the two million pounds really did exist, there was still a chance to save Harry. However slim the chance for a cure might be.

Harry's sickness had come on very suddenly. It had started with a few strange comments about his friend 'Lucas' and had progressed to wild tales about 'a blanket of snow covering the Earth.' Damien had no idea what delusions Harry was talking about and at first assumed his friend had started drinking again. But then, one day, after several bouts of severe headaches, Harry pointed at Damien and said, "You! You froze to death. What are you doing here? You're dead." Just as Damien was about to reply, to say that enough was enough, a violent gout of blood burst forth from Harry's nose and he collapsed to the ground unconscious.

The ambulance had arrived and carried Harry away. Twenty four hours and several tests later, doctors confirmed that he had a brain tumour. It was the reason for his bouts of confused babbling and manic delusions, and it was killing him.

Damien had wept, perhaps for the first and only time in his life. When his father had gone away to prison he had felt almost nothing, but the thought of Harry leaving was too much to bear. Despite having changed so much, Damien didn't think he could continue on the same path without Harry's guidance. He selfishly needed his friend to stay alive so that his own life was not upended back into the chaos he had only just managed to claw his way out of. Most of all, though, Damien couldn't face Harry dying because he loved the man. He was family. Harry was a father in the true sense of the word; not through biological potluck or obligation, but through genuine affection and loyalty.

I can't lose you, man. I have to get out of here.

Damien forwent his favoured drink of coffee and poured himself a cup of tea. He then took the steaming beverage over to the sofa and sat down in the spot where he had been sleeping for the last few hours. It was still warm.

For once, Danni had not slept beside him. He assumed that she was still feeling guilty about spinning the wheel when everybody else had decided not to. Although, as things turned out, it hadn't been a bad thing that she did. If there was a chance that somebody could get out of here alive, then what Danni did was fortuitous.

Although it could all just be a ruse to make us start participating in the games again.

Damien knew that there was still a large, even more likely possibility that all of them would still die inside the house, but they had nothing to lose by hoping otherwise. If Damien could just get the other bracelet off his wrist...

He took a sip of his tea and sighed as it relaxed him. It was a simple pleasure. He then took some time to study his fellow housemates – the final competitors.

Jade lay asleep in a star shape, legs and arms sprawled

outwards. She slept like she lived, loudly and with little regard for those around her. Richard lay beside her. His body was folded in, arms and ankles crossed. The racist piece of shit had fallen in line somewhat since their situation became more desperate, but Damien hadn't forgotten the man's true colours or what he had done to Lewis. Richard was a remorseless animal and that could not be forgotten. If anybody deserved to be here it was him.

Then there was Jules. What the woman had done to her sister was reprehensible, but was it due to malevolence or mere selfishness. From what he knew of Jules, she was an anxious, emotional person. Her insecurities may have been more to blame for her past actions than an actual desire to cause pain. Out of everybody who had had their sins exposed, hers were perhaps the most forgivable – the most human.

Maybe that's why Danni tried to palm the story off as her own.

Jules slept silently and still, more at peace than the nervous worrier that she was while awake. In fact, out of all of them, Jules was the only one who made no sound at all while she slept.

Jade's eyes fluttered and she was awake, staring directly ahead. Then she took in her surroundings and saw that Damien was awake as well.

"Morning," he said to her softly.

She smiled at him glumly while rubbing at her eyes with a balled up fist. "Morning. Did I miss anything?"

Damien shook his head. "I've only just woken up, but everybody's limbs seem to be attached, so no change yet."

Jade chuckled. "Ever get the feeling you took a wrong turn in life?"

"All the time, but not lately. I don't care what these

maniacs think I've done, I know that I deserve to live out the rest of my life. I've made mistakes in my life, but I've owned up to them. I don't answer to these tossers."

"Then who do you answer to?"

Damien shrugged. "My conscience. And right now it's clear."

"I hope one of us gets out of this alive," said Jade. She let out a long sigh. "And if it's me, I'm gonna make sure I bring these fuckers down."

Damien placed a finger against his lips. "Best keeping those intentions to yourself. You don't know what they can see and hear."

Jade nodded thoughtfully. Her usually impulsive nature seemed subdued this morning. "You're right," she said. "I've always needed to learn to keep my mouth shut. Perhaps I'll work on that if I get out of here."

"I think we would all do well to work on ourselves."

Damien went back to drinking his tea as Jade dozed off again. After a few minutes, Danni and Richard became awake, almost like a sixth sense told them that they were being watched.

Damien said, "Morning," to them both.

"Did I miss anything?" Danni asked.

Damien chuckled. "That's the exact same thing that Jade said when she woke up."

Danni smiled. "We must be developing a hive mind."

Richard stretched out his legs and then got up. "I'm going to go stick some toast on. Anybody want any?"

Nobody did.

"Suit yourselves."

"I fancy a cuppa," said Danni, getting up.

"I just boiled the kettle," said Damien. "Should still be warm."

Danni nodded and headed off into the kitchen. Jade had fallen back into a deep sleep and Jules was still unmoving. Damien watched her for a while and wished that he could sleep so serenely. His own slumber was full of fits and morbid dreams.

She looks so peaceful.

As he studied Jules, he had a strange feeling come over him. Her body was a little *too* still; her sleeping a little *too* restful.

"Hey, Jules," he said quietly. Then he said it a little louder. "Jules!"

Jade opened her eyes and looked at him. "Jeez, man!"

Damien smiled at her. "Sorry. I'm just trying to check if Jules is okay. She hasn't budged in a while."

Jade turned sideways on the sofa and faced Jules. "Hey, Jules," she said jarringly. "Yo! Jules, wake your lazy ass up!"

Jules remained still.

Damien leapt up from the sofa. "Oh fuck!"

He went over to Jules and grabbed her by both shoulders. He shook her vigorously.

There was no response. Jules head flopped left and right, but her eyes did not open.

Then Damien noticed the blood.

Between Jules's thighs, dark and drying on the sofa cushion was a vast bloodstain. It looked as though she had lost pints of the stuff. Her skin was almost white.

"She's dead," said Damien.

"You're shitting me," said Jade, leaping up from the sofa.

Damien shook his head and sighed. "Her internal injuries must have been worse than we thought. She must have been slowly dying since the task she was in."

"Least she went in her sleep," said Jade. "Maybe she didn't even know nothing about it."

"Perhaps. I hope so."

Damien went and informed Danni and Richard in the kitchen. They were both shocked. For one of them to die so quietly, amongst all of the dramatic death and chaotic torture, was a surprise.

"I just hope she'd made peace," said Danni. "She did a bad thing, but if she regretted it enough then she deserved forgiveness."

"None of that means shit," said Richard. "Dead is dead. There's no judgement, no redemption. We live our lives, good or bad, and then we die. Nothing we do matters worth a shit."

"I don't believe that," said Danni. "We carry our sins to the grave. Whether or not we die with a clear conscience makes a big difference."

"Not to me," said Richard, shoving a slice of buttered toast into his mouth and biting down.

Danni shrugged. She could see there was no point having a philosophical debate with the man. "So what should we do with her?"

"We're all in this together now. I say we put her somewhere peaceful."

Danni nodded. "Okay. We can put her in the bedroom with Catherine's body, but cover her with blankets and make it a little nicer for her."

"Okay. Sounds good. I think you and I should be able to manage on our own. She won't weigh much."

Damien took Jules's head while Danni took her bare legs. Together they transported her across the living area and towards the patio door. Jade helped out by sliding open the door for them.

The grass was wet as they stepped on it and Damien was

cautious not to slip. As he looked up at the sky, he felt sure it was going to rain again.

The door to the bedroom was hanging open. The dead, mutilated body of Patrick lay nearby and had started to smell. Damien wrinkled his nose in disgust.

I feel like I'm in Hell, surrounded by rotting flesh.

What makes me really frightened is how used to it I've gotten.

Damien and Danni shuffled through the bedroom door and approached the nearest bed. They eased Jules down onto the mattress respectfully and then stepped back.

"Should we say a few words?" Danni asked.

Damien shook his head. "What would be the point?"

He grabbed a couple of grimy blankets from some of the other beds and draped them over Jules. Danni helped him pull the sheets out so that they covered every inch of her.

"I think that's about as respectful as we can make it."

Damien nodded. "At least we tried."

"Promise you'll do the same for me...I mean, if it comes to it."

He looked at her and nodded. "I promise."

23

The Landlord's booming voice was due any moment, they all knew it; could even feel it in their bones probably. The routine of the house had become ingrained in them all and when something was about to happen they expected it, like a sixth sense.

I see dead people.

Couple of 'em are in the garden.

As expected, the speakers in the ceiling crackled. The Landlord began to speak.

"HOUSEMATES, I WOULD LIKE TO CONGRATU-LATE YOU ON COMING THS FAR. WITH THE UNFOR-TUNATE DEATH OF JULES, YOU ARE NOW THE FINAL FOUR CONTESTANTS. HALF OF YOU HAVE THE CHANCE TO LIVE, AT THE EXPENSE OF THE LIVES OF THE OTHERS. FOR SOME OF YOU, THESE WILL BE THE FINAL DAYS OF YOUR LIVES. FOR AT LEAST ONE OF YOU, THESE NEXT FEW DAYS WILL SIGNAL THE BEGINNING OF YOUR NEW PATH. YOU WILL BE REBORN AND RELEASED BACK INTO THE WORLD, BUT ONLY IF YOU ARE VICTORIOUS."

Damien scratched at his forehead and realised that he was sweating. He had survived so much already and now that an end was finally close, he felt like perhaps his luck would run out. Everything The Landlord said suggested that there was a way out of this house for somebody, but what if Damien ended up getting this far only to fail one of the final tasks? The thought was infinitely worse than if he had died in the very first task against Chris.

"THERE WILL BE NO TASK TODAY IN CELEBRATION OF YOU HAVING COME THIS FAR. THE PANTRY HAS BEEN FULLY STOCKED FOR YOU TO ENJOY. THE VIEWING SCREEN WILL BE DISPLAYING MOVIES FOR THE NEXT TWELVE HOURS. ENJOY YOURSELVES, HOUSEMATES. YOU HAVE EARNED IT."

Richard rolled his eyes. "The prick almost comes off as being benevolent."

"So, I guess we can relax for a while," said Jade.

Damien folded his arms. "It's just prolonging everything. I would prefer to just get this whole thing over with. I don't understand what there is to gain by waiting."

"What do you mean?" asked Danni.

"I mean, whose benefit is it for? If we're in here to play games and die, then why wait? Dragging it out suggests that there is something to gain by us being alive."

Danni frowned. "And what would that be?"

Damien thought about it, looked up at the nearest camera, and gave the only answer he could come up with, "Entertainment value."

"You think we really are being watched by an audience?"

Richard laughed. "Yeah, I bet we're on Comedy Central."

"Of course not," said Damien. "But perhaps we're part of some black market venture. People will pay for anything, believe me, I used to sell a lot of it. This could all be some black market game show to entertain sick fucks with fat bank accounts."

"They could be betting on us," said Jade. "Maybe that's how they fund it all. We get nominated and paid for by whoever feels wronged by us, and then the people running the show allow people to place bets on who will win the tasks."

"And who will win the entire thing," said Damien. "That would be the big pay off."

"Which would mean," said Jade. "That the promise of our lives is real. It would undermine the game to kill us all. The betting only makes sense if there is a true winner to bet on."

"Maybe they expect the two million to keep us quiet. They probably expect us to take the cash and just try and put the whole thing behind us."

"Doesn't sound like a bad idea," said Danni. "The house-mates who have died here are not worth the risk of us trying to expose everything. They were all bad people. If we win, we should just take the money and run."

Damien nodded. "I see what you're saying. The dead housemates were all pretty disgusting, for sure. That doesn't make this right, though. We're all human beings, not play things to be tortured and killed at the whim of those richer than us. I can't live in a world where that is okay."

"Then what?" said Richard. "You're going to bring this whole thing down to its knees? I'm sure it's that easy."

Damien shrugged. "Honestly I don't know what I'll do. But, even if the other housemates were evil and deserved what they got, these people have still fucked with me personally. I'm not sure I can let that go."

"Me either," said Richard. "But I'm sure the money will help."

"I'm not going to do anything," said Danni. "I just want to go back to my life. I'm not even supposed to be here."

"Yeah, me either," said Jade.

"No, really," said Danni. She went on to tell them all what she had told Damien, that her boss was the one who was supposed to be inside the house but she had impersonated her in order to change her life for the better.

"I applaud your balls," said Richard, "but things didn't really pay off for you there, did they?"

"That really sucks," said Jade. "I'm sorry you got caught up in all this with us sorry bunch of criminals."

"You don't know that we're criminals," said Richard. "We have no clue what each of us has done."

"I wouldn't say *no* clue," said Damien, pointing behind the sofa to the television. The silhouetted grid of faces had changed to display only a single line of four shadows now – one for each of the remaining housemates. Beneath the silhouettes were the final four remaining words: PEDDLER, MURDERER, TRAITOR, and CRUSADER.

Just as Damien had finished pointing at the screen, it switched over and displayed the opening credits to some movie. The jaunty soundtrack suggested a comedy, which was ironic as nobody would be in anywhere near the mood to enjoy it.

"Well," Jade said. "If people are watching, I'm going to give them a show. Let's go see what goodies are in the pantry. This might be my last chance to get shitfaced."

"Screw it!" said Damien. "Think I'll join you."

He followed Jade over to the pantry door and felt himself relax at the thought of having a drink. Despite the many ills of alcohol, nothing was quite as relaxing as a couple bottles of beer.

And that was exactly what they found inside the pantry:

bottles and bottles of Mexican beers, fresh limes, and several crates of beer; not to mention a huge bottle of tequila and a smaller one of scotch. But that wasn't all there was. Something else was inside the pantry.

24

D amien's eyes went wide. "Holy shitballs! Chris? You're alive?"

The former housemate, Chris, was trussed up inside the pantry. His eyes were glassy and afraid – the left one wasn't even moving. The many bruises that adorned his face suggested he had been through quite an ordeal.

Damien shook his head in confusion. *An ordeal that happened while he should have been dead.*

Jade reached into the pantry and yanked the gag out of Chris's mouth. He spluttered and coughed as he was suddenly able to breathe through his mouth again. His swollen nose must have been difficult to draw air in with.

"What are you doing here?" asked Damien. His skin was tingling with the sudden shock of seeing a dead man still alive and well.

Maybe not 'well' exactly, but alive at least.

When Chris spoke, he sounded timid and afraid, not at all like the brash Neanderthal he had been previously.

"The...the toxin didn't kill me. They...they used the counteragent to revive me before I was dead."

"Why?" said Damien. "Who?"

Chris shook his head and blinked. It was clear that his left eye was damaged as it remained stationary even as his other eye moved about freely.

"I don't know," he said. "I only spoke to that big guy in the black overalls. "He told me I was going to get another chance to win the game. He called me a 'wild card'."

Damien sighed. He reached into the pantry and started struggling with Chris's bonds. They were too tight.

"Can somebody go fetch me a knife," he said. "I need to cut him free."

Danni hurried and got Damien a knife from the kitchen, but even with the sharp blade it still took almost ten minutes to cut Chris loose and get him out of the pantry. They helped him over to the sofa and sat the poor guy down.

"I don't understand why they let you live," said Jade. "You were disqualified from the competition. The Landlord told us we were the remaining four contestants."

"Maybe he's in on all this," said Richard. "He went out first, without a mark on him."

Danni huffed. "I don't see what having a person on the inside would achieve. We're all under control and doing what we're told. Cameras cover our every move, I imagine, so why would they need a pair of eyes inside the house?"

"I don't know," said Richard, glaring down at Chris. "This just seems a bit fishy to me."

Damien laughed.

"What's so funny?"

"Nothing, you just never struck me as the type of guy to say 'a bit fishy'."

There was a brief moment of silence, but then Richard

cracked up laughing too. "You know what," he said. "That might just be the first time I ever said it."

Danni sat down beside Chris and patted him on the knee. "Did they tell you anything, Chris? Did they give you a reason for placing you back inside the house?"

Chris shook his head. "Just that I was being given another chance."

Damien folded his arms and chewed at his lip. He didn't like this. Chris was the biggest jerk in the house when this whole thing had started, even more so than Richard. Having him back inside with them would only mean bad things – and Richard's accusation of Chris being a part of what was going on was not entirely without merit either.

Damien unfolded his arms and sighed. "Alright, well, not a lot has changed. We still have a day to rest, so let's get the beers out. We can figure this all out later."

Jade headed back over to the pantry and returned with a six pack of *cervezas* and the bottle of tequila. "Let's get wasted," she said as she set them all down on the table. "There's plenty more when this is through."

Everyone settled down onto the sofa. Jade handed Chris a beer and he took it gladly. Damien took one for himself and enjoyed the crisp taste as it hit the back of his throat.

Danni was sitting beside him, a shot of tequila in her hand. She leant in close to him so that the others couldn't hear. "Do you think Chris is the traitor?"

Damien frowned at her. "Huh?"

"Murderer, peddler, crusader, *traitor*. Do you think that Chris could be the traitor?"

Damien shook his head. "No. He's the 'thug', remember? Before he arrived there was four of us left and four words on the screen."

"Then one of us is the traitor."

"What are you getting at? I'm more concerned about the fact that one of us is a murderer."

Danni sighed. "You're not understanding me. Maybe the traitor is here because of a betrayal in the past, but maybe they're betraying *us* right now. Maybe there really is someone on the inside."

"You mean like a *mole?*"

Danni nodded.

"Maybe. Like I said, though, I don't see the point. I think you're barking up the wrong tree. I think that Jade and Richard probably just screwed someone over in their past and that's why they're here. Anyway, Jade said she didn't trust *you* either. I guess we're all wondering who we can rely on."

Danni cleared her throat and took a sip of her tequila. "Perhaps you're right. I'm paranoid."

"It's not paranoia when someone is actually trying to kill you."

In fact it would be crazy not to be paranoid right now.

"What did they do to you?" Jade asked Chris. "You're all messed up."

Chris blinked and once again his left eye appeared dead and unmoving. "Most of it is due to whatever shit they shot into my wrists. When I woke up from the dose they gave me in the cube room I was blind in one eye and had the shakes. I still feel like I could drop dead at any minute – can feel it in my heart. The toxin has messed me up inside."

Jade cursed under her breath. "That sucks man. Least you ain't dead, though."

"May as well be."

"Is it true?" said Damien. "That you killed a guy at a football match."

Chris stared at Damien with his one good eye. "How you know about that?"

"They played a video after you were dead – when we thought you were dead. They play a video after anybody dies. It looks like the reason we're all in here is because someone on the outside wants to take revenge on us. Your video featured the father of the man you killed. Up until now, we've never had the chance to verify if the video accusations are true. So, is it true? Did you kill a guy?"

Chris nodded solemnly. "Didn't mean to. I'd had a shitload to drink and got into one of my moods. I was looking for trouble, but I went too far. I beat the guy to death. Not proud of it, but it's in my past. Can't say I think too much about it."

Damien shook his head. Chris's lack of regret was disgusting. "Well, it looks like the guy's father spent a lot of time thinking about it. He gave his life savings to get you in here."

Chris's face contorted. "That sonofabitch. If I ever get out of here... He better hope he dies of old age before I find him. I remember the old fucker in court, giving me the evils the whole time."

Damien huffed. "Can you blame him? You killed his son. You made his grandchildren orphans for no other reason than because you had too much to drink. You deserve everything you get."

Chris smirked. His bad eyes were watery and red. "So do you, else you wouldn't be here. Maybe you should leave your judgements to yourself because I honestly don't give a shit what you think."

Damien nodded. "You probably don't, but I promise you that you won't make it out of this alive. I'll happily die if it means taking you with me and away from that money."

Chris just laughed. "We'll see."

"Yeah," said Damien. "We will."

25

D amien had removed himself for the most part. Chris had seemed to regain some of his vitality after several bottles of beer, and he and Richard seemed to be having a grand old time as they laughed and hollered on the sofa. Jade was enjoying their company, too, but seemed to keep drifting off into her thoughts. Damien had noticed her several times staring into space.

Damien and Danni were sitting in the kitchen, sharing a bottle of red wine and sharing stories. Damien told her all about his friend, Harry, and how he was very sick. Danni had expressed her love for the theatre and did her best to convince Damien to try it one day if he ever got the chance. Her favourite show was *The Lion King*. He promised he would go see it.

"It's pretty noble you being here to help your friend," she said. "A much better reason than most of the other people in here, me included."

"You're not even supposed to be here," he said. "If anybody deserves to get out of this, it's you."

Danni stroked his forearm with the tips of her fingernails. "Thanks. It's terrible to say, but I hope both you and I get out of this."

Damien sighed. "I'd like to see us all get through this alive, but I suppose, if it's down to just two, then, yeah, I would like it to be me and you."

She leant forward and kissed him. Then she picked up her glass of wine and held it aloft. "Here's to you and me not dying."

Damien picked up his own wine and clinked it against her glass. "And to you and me going and getting a drink some place a lot nicer than this."

"Do you think Chris is going to be a problem?" she asked, her thoughts suddenly seeming to grow darker.

Damien nodded. "You can count on it. The guy is a psychopath."

"It looks like he and Richard are getting pretty close."

It was true. The men had been boozing together like a couple of old friends. They obviously understood that they were the pariahs of the group, but now that the numbers were so low, they had everything to gain by teaming up.

Damien cleared his throat and put down his glass. "That's because Richard knows he's on his own in here. No one has forgotten what he did to Lewis. The only person likely to condone that type of behaviour is Chris, so they make a good pair. In fact, they should fucking marry one another."

Danni topped up the wine glasses. "They're going to be much harder to deal with as a team. Chris being back could really hurt us."

Damien took a swig of his wine. He was beginning to really enjoy the taste. He might even prefer it to beer. "We'll take things as they come. Even if those two morons have each other's backs it doesn't matter, because you've got mine and I got yours."

"What about Jade?"

"I think she's starting to crumble. She hasn't been herself the last day or so. She's not even thinking about sides, but even if she was she would probably realise that she's the odd one out now that Chris has arrived."

Danni pulled some of her brown hair out of her face and looked over at Jade on the sofa who was still staring into space. "Too bad for her. She was doing so well."

"Yeah, she's a tough bird." Damien finished off the last of his wine and realised that the bottle was empty. He looked at Danni and raised his eyebrows. "Another?"

She nodded. "Of course."

Damien went over to the pantry and got another clutch of bottles. He placed two white in the fridge and took the remaining red one back to the counter. Danni unscrewed the top and began pouring.

"I'm glad I met you, Damien. If there's anything good to be gained from this whole thing, it's that."

"Likewise," said Damien. "Without you to talk to I think I might have gone insane."

Danni sipped her wine and then chuckled. "Give it chance. There's still time."

DAY 9

"GOOD MORNING HOUSEMATES. TODAY IS THE PENULTIMATE DAY OF THE COMPETITION. TODAY ONE OF YOU WILL DIE."

Damien felt his heart beating. With things being so close to an end, everything seemed much more imminent. The lack of housemates meant that the chances of him being involved in a grizzly task were much higher. There was a one in five chance today that he might die, and those odds were only going to get worse.

"WILL ALL HOUSEMATES KINDLY ENTER THE GARDEN AND AWAIT INSTRUCTION."

Everybody filed out into the garden. There was a light drizzle that threatened to get worse as thunder rumbled off in the distance. The sky above them was a brooding grey.

As if on cue, the courtyard platform began to rise, bringing with it the latest task for the housemates. This time the intended horror was clear.

"Oh God," said Danni. "They're sick. Totally sick! I'm not doing it."

Damien grabbed her shoulder and gave her a reassuring shake. You can do this. There'll be nothing to it."

Risen up out of the ground was a wooden shelf fixed horizontally at head height. Affixed at spaced intervals were five glass bowls like old fashioned fish tanks, only much larger. At the bottom of each bowl was an opening covered by a folded leather flap. Inside each of the bowls were hundreds of swarming wasps.

"PARTICIPATION IN THIS TASK IS MANDATORY. INSIDE EACH OF THE GLASS BOWLS IS A COLONY OF SAXON WASPS. THEY HAVE BEEN AROUSED BY A CHEMICAL PHEROMONE AND ARE CURRENTLY IN ATTACK MODE. THE TASK AHEAD OF YOU IS AS FOLLOWS... PLACE YOUR HEADS INSIDE THE GLASS BOWLS. THE FIRST TWO PEOPLE TO REMOVE THEIR HEADS WILL PERFORM IN TONIGHT'S ELIMINATION TASK. PLEASE BEGIN."

Damien swallowed a lump in his throat and stared at the buzzing fury in front of him. The yellow and black blur was an embodiment of ferocity. Their hundreds of tiny bodies made up a single attacking organism. And he was about to shove his face right in the middle of it.

"I don't think I can do this," said Danni. "In fact I can't."

"You have to," said Damien. "Or else you'll end up in the elimination task and might die."

"You'll die now," said Jade. "The Landlord said this task was mandatory. That means anyone who refuses gets the cuffs."

Danni shook her head and looked like she was close to freaking out. Damien held her hand. "I can hold onto you from here," he said. "Just close your eyes and take deep breaths. I promise I will get you through this."

Danni looked at him. Her dark eyes were like saucers. But she nodded. "Okay."

The five housemates stood in a line, looked at one another and then crouched below the leather flaps at the bottom of the bowls.

"After three," said Jade. "One...two...three..."

All five housemates shoved their heads into the glass bowls. There was no screaming, just terrified silence broken only by buzzing. Damien closed his eyes and gritted his teeth, making sure to close up any entry into his body that the wasps could exploit.

The stinging began immediately.

Damien gritted his teeth harder as one sting became several became dozens. The pain was not at first agonising, but as the number of insect attacks increased, the throbbing in his cheeks, forehead, and neck tripled. The discomfort was added to by the repulsion of a thousand little legs creeping over his flesh.

Screw this!

Damien yanked his head down through the leather flap and leapt away. He batted at his face with both hands and spat and blinked fitfully.

He realised that everybody else was doing the same. There was nobody left with their head still inside the bowl and everyone was moving about the lawn and batting at their heads in the same way as him.

Danni looked up at him with a glowing red face. Her upper eyelid was swollen and a little black speck marked her. She looked truly miserable.

Damien approached her, ignoring the burning agony that engulfed his own face. "Hold still," he said.

Danni stopped wriggling and kept her weeping eyes on him.

Damien reached out a hand and moved his fingers toward her face. "Don't move and don't blink." He grasped the stinger between his thumb and forefinger and plucked it from Danni's eyelid.

She flinched.

Damien held the insect appendage in front of her. "It was stuck in your eyelid."

Danni groaned. Her lips were fat and swollen, like she'd had a collagen injection. "That really sucked," she said.

"I know. But who pulled out first? When I pulled out and opened my eyes, everybody else was out too."

Danni shrugged.

"HOUSEMATES JADE AND DANNI. YOU WILL BE IN TONIGHT'S HEAD TO HEAD ELIMINATION."

"Guess that answers your question," said Danni. "Looks like it's finally my turn."

26

Danni and Jade were standing outside the door to the elimination chamber and waiting for the go ahead. Danni was holding herself nervously, so Damien went over to give her a pep talk.

"Just keep a level head and you'll be fine. Jade is erratic, you can benefit from that."

"If I benefit then that means Jade dies."

"If you don't, then you die."

Danni nodded. Her face was still very swollen from the wasp stings. She had the features of someone six stones heavier. "Good point. I feel really sick."

Damien put his hands on her shoulders. "Just breathe slowly. Don't think about anything but what you're doing right now."

"HOUSEMATES DANNI AND JADE, PLEASE ENTER THE ELIMINATION CHAMBER."

Danni gave Damien a last fleeting look and smiled. "Here I go. Wish me luck."

"Good luck."

Damien went and took a seat on the sofa. He could see

everything inside the cube room via the viewing screen in the living area.

Danni and Jade stood in the white room, side by side. In front of them was a large metal disc. It was a circular saw. Damien groaned when he spotted it. On the floor next to it, hooked through a series of steel rings, was a sturdy rope.

"HOUSEMATES DANNI AND JADE, PLEASE PICK UP THE ROPE IN FRONT OF YOU FROM OPPOSITE ENDS."

Reluctantly, the two women did as they were asked. They held the rope up between them like they were about to engage in tug-of-war.

The metal saw disc started spinning. After a few slow revolutions it kicked into gear and became a lethal blur of sharp teeth.

"HOUSEMATES, THE GAME IS SIMPLE. PULL YOUR OPPONENT INTO THE CENTER OF THE ROOM. PLEASE BEGIN."

Jade and Danni just stood there and stared at one another with terror-filled eyes. Then Jade yanked the rope. Danni went stumbling forward, towards the spinning blade.

Damien lurched to the edge of his seat in the living area and let out an anxious breath.

Danni managed to stop herself just in time. Less than half a foot away from the saw blade she managed to dig in her heels and pull back on the rope. Jade stumbled forwards in response and the two women were back to where they started.

Both of them started to pull and strain, the effort making their already red faces turn beetroot within seconds. They were in a physical battle for their lives.

"Come on, Jade," Chris shouted. "Give that skinny bitch a ride on the wheel."

Damien stood up from the sofa and faced Chris who was standing behind it. "I'd be quiet if I were you."

Chris just smirked.

Jade began to gain a slight advantage and Danni started to slide along the floor. Her bare feet kept turning and adjusting as she tried to gain purchase, but she was slowly losing.

Jade's teeth showed as she grunted with effort. She yanked the rope like a dog with a chew toy. The more she began to gain a few steps, the more determined she seemed to get. The fact that she was pulling an innocent woman to her death was apparently not in her mind.

Danni gritted her teeth and leant back, almost horizontal. She managed to get the rope going the other way. Jade began to slip and slide; she lost her footing and fell down to her bottom.

Danni yanked harder and dragged Jade to within inches of the whirring blade. Her eyes stretched wide as she stared into the spinning death.

Jade managed to pull back a few feet and a stalemate ensued. Both women groaned and huffed as they fought desperately to gain an inch on their opponent.

Damien and the others watched breathlessly from the other room. Even Chris had his mouth shut.

Jade yanked, Danni stumbled.

Danni got a grip.

Danni yanked.

Jade stumbled.

"HOUSEMATES DANNI AND JADE, YOU HAVE THREE MINUTES TO DECIDE A VICTOR OR BOTH OF YOU WILL DIE."

Neither women could afford to show a reaction to The Landlord's statement, but the increased effort showed on their faces. They had now gone bright purple and their eyeballs bulged.

Jade was the first to slip. One of her ankles turned inwards and she lost her purchase. Danni took advantage and summoned the last of her strength reserves. Jade slid on her heels, unable to dig in. The spinning saw blade got closer and closer.

Jade managed to strike her heels into the ground just a few inches away from the lethal metal teeth. She looked at Danni, her eyes wide and pleading, her chest heaving in and out. "Please!" she said.

Then Danni gave the rope one final yank and Jade went stumbling forward.

Watching the viewing screen, Damien cried out in horror. He had expected the blade to saw Jade clean in two, but it didn't. Jade fell onto the blade and it quickly hollowed out her insides. Her head and neck and waist and legs remained intact, but her middle was gone. She slumped to the floor with the saw blade continuing to spin inside of her. It almost looked like a part of her torso.

The bracelet on Danni's right hand snapped open and fell to the floor.

27

D anni came out of the elimination chamber covered in blood. She had a faraway gaze on her face that suggested she may have lost a part of herself to the horror. Damien led her over to the sofa and gently sat her down. Jade's video had already begun to play on the television screen.

"My brother was stabbed twenty nine times and left to rot on the bathroom floor," said a middle-aged woman with brown hair greying around the temples. "His head was almost hanging off. I knew that Jade was the one who did it. She was a manipulative bitch from the day my brother met her. They argued and fought all the time if she didn't get her way, and I had seen her lose her temper several times. All the drugs they were doing together just made things worse. When Jade had been doing coke, her temper was insane. She's the only one who could have killed my brother.

But the police found nothing to stick. They found the knife but no fingerprints. They caught Jade out in a few lies, but nothing conclusive. The fact that she was high all the time meant that anything she said could not be verified one way or the other. No one was ever brought to trial and my brother's murder is still unsolved – officially. I know that Jade did it, though. And now she's going to face my trial...my punishment."

The viewing screen went blank. The Landlord's voice came over the speakers.

"CONGRATULATIONS REMAINING HOUSEMATES, TOMORROW IS YOUR FINAL DAY INSIDE THIS HOUSE. SOME OF YOU WILL DIE, SOME OF YOU WILL GO FREE. GOOD LUCK AND SLEEP WELL."

DAY 10

Everyone worked together at breakfast to fry up sausages, eggs, bacon, toast, and mushrooms. For some of them – perhaps all of them – it could be their final meal. They all ate their morning feast in silence.

They all felt the loss of Jade harder than any of the other housemates. She had been loud and ever-present, the mouth of the house. Her loss was a silent hole in the atmosphere.

Can't believe she was a cold blooded murderer, Damien thought. *I had her more pegged as a reformed drug addict or a thief. Well, maybe what happened was what got her straight. Maybe she was trying to put the past behind her.*

Well, guilty or not, at least I can stop worrying who the 'murderer' is. All that's left is the 'peddler', the 'crusader', and the 'traitor'. I wonder which one is Danni and which one is Richard?

"I wonder how long we have," said Danni, placing down her knife and fork on her empty plate. "I mean until the tasks begin."

Richard shrugged. "Not long I suppose. I didn't sleep a

wink last night. Think it's the first time I've ever been afraid."

"That's quite an admission," said Damien. "You're not really the vulnerable type."

"Don't get me wrong," he said. "I plan on leaving you all for dead, but I can't help but freak out about what I've just lived through and what's still left ahead of me. There's no way to truly survive this thing. Even the winners can't exactly just go back to their old lives like nothing happened. This crap will stain our souls forever."

"Maybe that's the point," said Damien. "Maybe we're supposed to learn a lesson and be better people than we were."

Richard nodded his head, almost imperceptible, and then went to say something, but Chris cut him off.

"When I get out of here, I'm going to be rich – with balls of steel to boot. Surviving this thing is going to make me feel like a fucking legend; walking away when everyone else is dead…pretty epic!"

Danni huffed. "I guess some of us aren't capable of changing."

Chris shrugged. "Some of us don't want to. Who gets to decide what's right and wrong? We're all born on this earth the same way and it's up to us what the fuck we do with our lives. Just because someone wears a uniform and tells me something is the law don't make it so, as far as I'm concerned. I never once agreed to live by anybody else's rules. I never agreed to pay taxes or obey the law. Other people just made that assumption. I do what the hell I want with my life and I'll be damned if I'm ever going to feel bad about it."

"You know," said Damien. "There's something liberating about what you say, Chris. Maybe we should all follow our own moral compasses and do what we personally feel is right. The problem is that you have the moral compass of a brain damaged Hitler."

Chris grinned. "I'll take that as a compliment."

"Take it any way you want. Just know that the world will be a better place without you."

"World would be better without a lot of things, mate. Shame life ain't perfect, nor is it ever likely to be."

"Not as long as people like you are in it, no."

"Weren't you a bit of scumbag once?" Richard commented. "So who are you to judge?"

Damien nodded. "But I was a scumbag by circumstance, not by choice. When push came to shove I took a better path."

"Good for you," said Chris. "And yet your path led you to the exact same place as mine. Guess that would be proof that nothing we do matters, so might as well do whatever we feel like."

Damien said nothing.

"Seems like he's finally run out of self-righteous juice," said Chris, nudging Richard in the ribs and laughing. Richard joined in the laughter but seemed to be hiding some sort of regret behind his eyes. Maybe the guy had actually done some thinking and didn't like the conclusions he had come to.

Damien still chose to say nothing. There was no need for words any longer. The only thing that mattered now were the tasks ahead. He could deal with Richard and Chris simply by winning.

"HOUSEMATES, TODAY THERE WILL BE NO ELIMINATION TASKS, ONLY A FINAL GROUP TASK THIS EVENING. THIS WILL DETERMINE THE VICTOR."

Richard and Chris whispered something to one another and then nodded conspicuously.

Damien did the same with Danni. "Those two are going to be working together. We should do the same."

"Of course. You don't even have to say so. I have your back."

Damien smiled and kissed Danni on the cheek. "That means a lot to me."

"Shall we head to the garden? That's usually where the fun and games take place."

Damien nodded. They left Richard and Chris conspiring in the kitchen and went out into the garden. It was raining moderately but it wasn't a problem. The days of worrying about things as mundane as comfort were long gone.

Damien took a seat on one of the perimeter's benches. Danni stood in front of him and stroked her fingers through his hair. Nothing was said between them. They both just held each other in the rain as they waited for their fates to begin.

28

Night had fallen and spotlights came on and lit the garden as the platform began to rise. Damien and Danni were both still together, sitting side by side on the bench and leaning in against one another. The mutual warmth and the comfort of having each other near had lulled Damien into a relaxed daze. He quickly snapped out of it when he saw the platform coming up out of the ground.

Here we go. Return to Thunderdome.

"HOUSEMATES, ASSEMBLE IN THE GARDEN."

Chris and Richard strolled out from inside the house, both of them smiling confidently.

"Let the games begin," Chris said, grinning. "I think I owe you one, Damien, after our first head to head."

Damien nodded. "Try not to get disqualified this time."

"Don't worry. I'm going to be winning this one."

On the platform was a wooden tool rack. On the rack were four handheld axes, not much bigger than hatchets.

"HOUSEMATES, EACH OF YOU MUST PICK UP AN

AXE AND THEN RETREAT TO A CORNER OF THE GARDEN."

Danni looked at Damien nervously. "I don't like this."

Damien sighed. "Me either. Come on, let's just go along for now."

All four housemates marched up to the platform and took one of the hand axes from the rack. Then they each picked a corner and retreated to it.

"ALL OF YOU HAVE DONE WELL TO BE HERE. YOU HAVE BEATEN YOUR OPPONENTS IN VARIOUS ENCOUNTERS AND HAVE PROVEN YOURSELF WORTHY. YOU ARE WARRIORS. NOW YOU MUST FIGHT FOR YOUR ULTIMATE SURVIVAL. TO WIN, YOU MUST MURDER TWO OR ALL OF THE REMAINING HOUSEMATES. YOU HAVE THE TOOLS AT YOUR DISPOSAL, NOW USE THEM. GOOD LUCK."

Damien stared down at the axe in his hands with disbelief. This whole thing had been a nightmare from the beginning, and many people were dead, but Damien had not been made to directly take the life of another until now. There had been competitions where he'd needed only to focus on winning. Now he was being told to actively murder his opponent.

I can't do it.

Danni screamed. Damien looked up and over at her.

Chris was hurrying towards her without a shred of remorse as she cowered and begged in her corner of the courtyard.

He's going to hack her to pieces.

Damien bolted, racing across the grass. He had to get to Danni before Chris did or she was dead.

But there was no way he was going to make it. Chris had had too much of a head start.

He's going to kill her. Then those two bastards are going to team up and come after me.

Chris came within feet of Danni who was cowering on her knees. If she hadn't clammed up in terror, she might have been able to get away, but the danger had frozen her in place.

Chris reared back with the axe, ready to strike.

Without thinking, Damien raised his own axe from several yards away. Then he flung it as hard as he could. The weapon tumbled and spun through the air towards its target.

The weapon struck Chris in the side of his head. It didn't embed itself like in the action movies. It just *thunked* against his skull and fell to the floor.

Danni screamed in fright as Chris hit the ground. His head had been split open and a wide open gash travelled from the top of his skull all the way down behind his ear. He lay on the ground convulsing and yelping. The axe might not have sliced his head in two, but the blunt force trauma alone had been enough to put the man down.

Damien made it over to Danni and dragged her upwards to her feet. "Come on," he said. "Snap out of it."

Richard was standing near the centre of the garden. He had been watching what had happened and seemed worried. His partner had been taken out of the game and suddenly the numbers were not in his favour.

Richard held his hands up and smiled. "Hey man. We can't go around killing each other just because of their say so. You ain't no killer, man."

Damien glanced down at Chris who was on his back and staring up at the sky dazedly. His breathing was irregular and laboured.

"Well," said Damien. "In a couple of minutes when Chris is dead, I *will* be a killer."

Richard nodded and an atmosphere of mutual understanding formed in the air. They each understood the situation. There was no compromise to be had.

Chris moaned on the floor, still dying.

"This is pretty screwed up, huh?" said Richard.

Damien nodded. "That's an understatement."

Richard sniffed, readjusted the grip on his hand axe. "We're going to have to go for it, aren't we?"

"'Fraid so. Sorry."

Richard threw his axe to the ground at his feet and shrugged his shoulders. "Tell you the truth, I probably deserve it."

Damien frowned. "What are you doing?"

Richard got down on his knees. "Taking responsibility for the things I've done. Just do it. Make it quick."

Damien took a few steps forward, but kept the axe by his side. "You can't just give up. That's suicide."

Richard nodded. "I guess. Tell you the truth, I was contemplating it anyway. The reason I signed up to be here was because my life sucked. You two should take the money. I don't deserve it. You've already seen the kind of man I am. I'm full of anger and violence. To be honest, I'm tired of feeling that way. I never meant to be the man I am, but.... Well, there's not much else to say, so just get it over with."

Damien took another step forward, raised the axe above his head. But lowered it again. He looked at the painting of the eyeball and felt like it was watching him. "I can't just kill you, man. It's not right."

Richard looked up at Damien and nodded.

Then he sucker punched him right in the nuts.

Damien hunched over and fell backwards, stars

clouding his vision as all of the air was forced from his lungs. Richard grabbed his axe back up off the floor and stalked after him, ready to swing the axe.

Damien tried to catch his breath, put a hand up to protect himself.

Rage contorted Richard's face as he chopped the axe downwards.

Damien closed his eyes and waited to be cut open.

Something struck Richard from the side and his swing went wide. He staggered to his right and dropped the axe on the floor again. There was a confused, disbelieving look on his face and it soon became clear what had happened.

Danni knelt down beside Damien, a bloody axe in her hand. Damien looked over and saw the blood begin to spray from Richard's neck as his hacked-up jugular ruptured. The guy dropped to his knees and tried to stem the wound with both hands, but it was no use. His face was already beginning to grow pale as Death sharpened his scythe in anticipation.

Damien was still in agony. A wave of nausea had taken over him and he was taking deep breaths to try and send it away. His whole midsection ached as pulses of dull, throbbing pain emanated from his groin.

"Are you okay?" Danni asked him.

Damien huffed and puffed. "Yeah...are you?"

She smiled at him. "I'm great. This thing should finally be over now. We made it."

Damien looked left and looked right. Richard and Chris were both slowly bleeding to death. They would each be dead within the next few minutes.

"HOUSEMATES DANNI AND DAMIEN, CONGRATULATIONS. YOU ARE THE VICTORS. PLEASE ASSEMBLE IN THE LIVING AREA."

29

Damien managed to catch his breath after the blow to his testicles and was now sitting on the sofa anxiously. Was this really all over? Even if it was, would he really be allowed to walk free? Would he be given the money he was promised?

A million quid each for me and Danni?

Enough to give Harry a chance.

Danni leant into Damien and he put his arm around her. She said, "We did it. We stuck together and we made it to the end."

Damien kissed the top of her head. "Yeah, we did. We made it."

But at what cost?

"HOUSEMATE DANNI, HOUSEMATE DAMIEN, THE COMPETITION IS NOW OVER. PLEASE ENTER THE ELIMINATION CHAMBER."

Damien groaned. "Thought I'd seen the last of that place."

"Me too. Maybe that's where they're going to let us out."

Damien stood up and took Danni by the hand, while also picking up the hand axe he had left on the sofa. He felt better with it. Together the two of them walked towards the elimination chamber door, two survivors ready to leave a warzone.

Damien held the door open for Danni and they both stepped into the white cube room. It was a place of death and suffering, but perhaps now it was the room where their salvation would take place.

In the centre was a long metal table. There were two large open briefcases, one at either end. Between them, in the centre, was a large red button.

Damien stared at the two briefcases on the table and actually let out a whistle. They were both filled with piles and piles of money, stacked neatly in thick wads of fifties.

"That's a fuck load of money."

Danni looked at him and grinned. "You're telling me. I guess this whole thing was legit after all. They're giving us two million pounds."

Damien suddenly felt lighter. More and more he was beginning to believe that he might just get out of this thing alive. But there was just one thing he didn't yet understand.

What's that button for?

"HOUSEMATES, CONGRATULATIONS. BEFORE YOU IS TWO MILLION POUNDS IN CASH. IT IS YOURS TO SHARE EQUALLY. YOU ARE ALSO FREE TO LEAVE THIS HOUSE THROUGH A DOOR THAT WILL SOON OPEN."

Damien and Danni exchanged glances and smiled.

"HOWEVER, YOU HAVE ONE FINAL DECISION AHEAD OF YOU. ON THE TABLE IS A BUTTON. PRESS IT AND YOU WILL RECEIVE 100% OF THE MONEY. YOU

WILL NOT BE REQUIRED TO SHARE. PRESS THE
BUTTON ON THE CENTRE OF THE TABLE AND YOUR
FELLOW HOUSEMATE WILL DIE, LEAVING YOU ALL
THE CASH."

Damien sighed. "That's messed up," he said. "We're not
about to betray each other after all that we've been through.
A million each is more than-"

Danni sprinted over the table and pressed down on the
button with both hands.

Damien had remained rooted to the spot for the single
second it had taken for Danni to betray him. His mouth was
hanging open. He did not understand.

Danni turned around and faced him from the table. Her
remaining bracelet sprung open and clattered to the floor.
She was finally free.

Damien shook his head at her. "W-why?"

Danni grinned. She was suddenly very ugly and
distorted, like a complete stranger. "Richard was the 'crusader,'" she said. "He burned down a mosque in Leeds and tried
to incite a local race war. "And it's pretty obvious that you're
the 'peddler,' what with all the poison you helped push on
desperate people that needed help more than they needed a
line of coke. So, who does that leave?"

Damien sighed. "Traitor."

Danni smirked at him. "Pity you figured it out a little
late. It's been fun playing you like a fiddle."

"What? Are you saying that you were a part of this?"

"Duh!"

"But why? What was the point of you pretending to be
like the rest of us?"

She rolled her eyes. "Why do you think? I'm here to
make sure that no one walks away the winner. Can't have

you spilling the beans, can we? You can call me the contingency plan if you like. Oh, don't get me wrong. You're the winner, but as for letting you walk free, that just can't happen."

Damien couldn't make it add up in his brain. "But the tasks, the games... Why put this money in front of me if it was all just a scam."

Danni held her bandaged hand up in front of her. She unravelled it to show that she had no injuries – no acid burn. "The wasp stings sucked pretty bad, but all of the other tasks were faked. There was only water in my bowl during the acid task. The task I was in with Jade was weighted in my favour. There was a slight incline to the floor that gave me a little helping hand from gravity. Of course I made it look close, but it never really was. As for the money, well that's payment for me and my team. We're a cash only kind of organisation. Every time we do this, we get a couple suitcases of cash sent down from the people running things." She ran a hand over the money in the suitcases. "God, how I love payday."

Damien snarled. "You bitch!"

"Hey, I'm one of the good guys. All of you deserved to be here. You're the scum of the earth."

Damien shook his head. "No. I changed."

"Perhaps, but there's a kid called Gaz Brown that hasn't walked since the day you beat him to a pulp. Poor kid doesn't even know what day it is."

Damien sighed, and then actually laughed to himself.

"What?" Danni asked. "What's so funny?"

"I didn't lay a finger on Gaz Brown. My father was responsible. He just let me take the street cred for it. You got your facts wrong."

"We never get our facts wrong. Gaz Brown's father paid a lot of money to see you held responsible."

"Well, sorry to break it to you, but he's got the wrong guy." Damien tightened his grip on the axe in his hand. "And now I'm going to hold you responsible for the fuck up."

He ran at Danni but only made it half way. An unbearable burst of agony shot through his left wrist. Immediately he dropped the axe and keeled over. The pain took over him in waves. His diaphragm seized up and his mouth filled with saliva. The steel collar sprung free of his neck, any chance for the counter-agent gone.

Danni came and stood over him. "Nobody ever gets out of here alive. I'm very good at what I do."

Damien stared up at her and gritted his teeth. "I'm... going to...kill you."

"Not in this life."

Damien used the last of his strength to grab the hand axe from the floor beside him.

Danni's eyes went wide. She leapt back and put several feet of space between them. Then she began to laugh. "You idiot. You'll be dead within minutes and yet you still fight."

Damien grimaced, but managed to pull a smirk across his face. "The axe wasn't meant for you."

Before Danni could realise what he meant, Damien chopped the axe against his left wrist. The flesh and tendons split apart and fragile bones broke.

He chopped again.

Then one more time, as hard as he could manage before shock sent him weak.

Damien's left hand slithered across the floor as his arm came away from it. The bracelet that had circled his wrist fell to the floor and leaked a yellowish liquid that must have been the toxin.

Danni's eyelids were stretched wide open, making her eyes look like marbles inside her head. "Get me out of here," she shouted and backed up towards the opposite wall. "The fool's lost his mind."

Two large men immediately entered the room through a hidden back door. They bundled Danni through it to safety and then started towards Damien. One of the men was the big fucker in black overalls.

Damien's head was spinning. He felt sick and close to unconsciousness, but he had to get away.

He managed to get up off the floor and stagger backwards, keeping his eyes on the two approaching men, while making his way to the door that led back into the house. In his right hand, he still held the axe but it felt unbearably heavy in his hand.

The two guards said nothing. They just stalked after him with murderous intent. The man in the black overalls was smiling.

Damien reached behind himself and fumbled for the door handle. He found it and was relieved when it turned.

The men picked up their pace. Damien fell backwards through the door back into the house. He landed on his rump, but quickly got himself together and kicked the door closed again, before the two larger men could come through it.

He sat on the floor, axe held ready in his hand, eyes on the door.

The door remained closed.

The two men were not following.

Why aren't they coming in here to get me?

Damien looked down at the gushing stump where his hand used to be and knew the answer.

I'm bleeding to death. They don't need to come after me. They can just wait until I die.

Damien managed to prop himself up on his one hand and slowly climb to his feet. He took a deep breath and tried to keep his mind from spinning.

I'm not dead yet, you ass hats.

Damien turned on the spot, looking for a way to preserve his life. It didn't take him long before he found one.

He stumbled over into the kitchen and placed himself in front of the cooker. With his right hand he twisted the knob for the gas hob and pressed the clicker to ignite the flame. The lower left hob hissed and then lit up with a bright blue flame that slowly turned orange.

Damien began to hyperventilate but caught himself just in time, before he went into full blown panic. He watched the flame with grim fascination. The destructive force of fire might possibly be about to become a life saver.

Damien shoved the bleeding stump of his left arm over the naked flame and screamed as he forced himself to hold it there. Every automatic impulse firing from his brain ordered him to remove his flesh from the burning agony, but he fought it. He fought it for almost twenty seconds before he flopped backwards against the cabinets behind him and slid to the floor in a gibbering daze.

He stared down at his stump to see that it was blistered and blackened. But it was no longer bleeding. His veins, arteries, and capillaries had been cauterised. He was no longer bleeding to death. Infection would probably be the thing to kill him now.

But not for a while. I have time for a little payback.

Damien reached up from the floor and rummaged

around in the drawer above his head. His hand came back with a 12-inch chef's knife held firmly in its grip.

They would be coming to get him, Damien knew, but this time he was ready for them. It was time for the owners of this house to play one of *his* games.

And it's a game you're going to lose, Mr Fucking Landlord.

30

D amien had grown thirsty. He didn't know how long he'd been slumped on the kitchen floor but it seemed like a while – maybe hours.

He climbed up off the floor and bent himself over the sink. Turning on the tap, he placed his mouth beneath the faucet and then gulped and gulped until he was out of breath. He let out a gasp and wiped his mouth.

Right, so what's the plan? I might be free of those damned bracelets, but I'm still inside the belly of the beast.

Damien looked around the kitchen and managed to find a spare bandage from the first aid kits they'd been given during earlier tasks. He wrapped up the burnt stump of his left wrist and yelled out as a fresh burst of pain reignited itself.

He rooted around the kitchen until he found half a bottle of whiskey and quickly unscrewed the cap. He downed the entire contents. The spirit burned his throat and made him gag, but the warm fuzz immediately flowed through his veins and made the pain in his wrist melt away.

Damien picked up the chef's knife from the counter and took it over to the heavy metal door where he and the other housemates had originally entered the nightmare of the house. As he expected, it was locked tight, impenetrable.

Next, he checked the doors for the pantry and the elimination chamber. Both had been locked from the other side.

They've caged me up in here. Left me to rot.

There were no other doors that Damien could try. He kicked and hefted his shoulder against the pantry door but it wouldn't budge. Unless he chanced upon a sledgehammer, he would never get the door open. For all he knew, Danni and her cohorts could be locking the place down right now, deserting ship. He would be trapped inside for days as he slowly starved to death or died of infection.

I can't let it end that way. I have to get out of here.

Damien was feeling better as the whiskey saturated his system. He was confident and relaxed, but he was also a little fuzzy. Despite the slight inebriation, he was still crystal clear about one thing: The longer he was trapped inside the house, the less chance he had of getting to the people responsible for putting him there.

Maybe I can get out through the bedroom.

Damien headed out into the rain-soaked garden and trudged across the courtyard into the bedroom. The smell of death hit him immediately. Catherine's body had been stagnating for several days now and Jules had joined her not long ago.

Damien pulled his hoodie up over his nose to keep away the stench. Catherine's face had turned a mottled alabaster with sickly patches of purple. The wrinkled skin of her old face had begun to slide back as though it were making a break for the back of her skull. Damien had never seen a decomposing body before and he would gratefully have this be the last time.

And if I don't get out of here, the same thing is going to happen to me.

It didn't take long before it became clear that there were no points of egress inside the bedroom. Not a single door or window had been built into the walls. Escape via there was not even a possibility.

Not wanting to be around the dead housemates any longer, Damien headed back out into the garden. The sight of Patrick's body in the far corner made him sigh. There was death everywhere. It seemed even more pervasive now that his was the only heartbeat left in the house. He was alone in a mausoleum.

There has to be something I can do. I just need to think.

He scanned the garden and thought about trying to scale the walls. It might be doable if he tried stacking up furniture and climbing the ten-feet to the top, but the thick layers of razor wire would have made it impossible to make it over to the other side. He would be cut open like a peach against a cheese grater.

He peered up at the sky and let the rain caress his face. The rhythmic patter allowed him to focus inwards, to put his thoughts in order. It was almost like he was connecting with some calming, intangible force that sought only to inspire him.

Perhaps that's what God is.

Eventually something occurred to Damien. There was maybe just one single way that he could escape the house; one last exit that he hadn't tried. And he was standing right next to it.

The raised platform that had brought the housemates

the axes with which to kill each other was still in its upright position. The fact that it had risen almost every day with different equipment on it suggested that it led to another area of the facility, and therefore would lead to a way out.

Damien hurried over to the platform and stood inside the compartment that had housed the hand axes. If he could just find a way to make the platform descend, it would take him out of the courtyard to some place new. But there were no controls or buttons that he could see to operate the pneumatic platform.

Damn it.

The platform had two girders on either side that held the patch of grass above which provided its disguise when the platform was lowered. Running up both girders was a coarse black wire. Damien prodded the wires and discovered that they were firm, yet slightly pliant. Their sponginess suggested that the rubber shielding housed not copper wires or fibre optics, but something else: gas or air.

It's part of the pneumatics. The air pumps through these cables and lowers and raises the platform.

Damien tried to pinch the cables closed, but they were too strong. Then a better idea occurred to him.

Damien realised that he still held the chef's knife in his hand. He held it up in front of him. Then he slashed at one of the cables. Immediately there was a hiss of air. Damien slashed at the cable again and it split apart, the two severed ends pointing in separate directions.

The platform grumbled and shifted.

Damien spun around and slashed at the remaining cable.

More air hissed. The platform began to move. It tilted and then settled, before easing downwards as if sinking through a vat of custard. The ground beneath Damien's feet descended slowly. He used the time to prepare for whatever came next. The last thing he saw was the great staring eye painted on the wall beneath the spotlights.

31

The platform came to a stop inside some sort of staging area. The ground was bare cement and an oily odour clung to the air. It was not unlike an empty garage.

The only things inside the room were several tiers of metal shelving that housed a variety of equipment. Amongst the equipment were petrol cans, batteries, containers, cattle prods, folded-up tables, the large 'wheel of fortune', and more hand axes like the ones used to kill Chris and Richard.

Damien exchanged his chef's knife for one of the axes, but decided to keep the blade spare. He slid it into his waist band at the back beneath his hoodie. He then trained his eyes on the doorway ahead. It was hanging open.

That's good, because I was getting really sick of locked doors.

Damien took a step and wobbled as the whiskey in his system started to play havoc with his motor controls. The alternative was being sober and feeling the full blown agony from his wrist. He accepted that the grogginess was a neces- sary evil.

Passing through the doorway up ahead, he found

himself inside a warehouse area. Various pallets were stacked up with machinery and various other things. There were also huge stockpiles of booze and snacks. Much more than twelve housemates could consume in ten days. A forklift truck sat abandoned in the centre of the warehouse and several hard hats hung from a nearby wall. It was quite an operation.

What the hell is this place? It can't just be about a handful of people with a grudge. This place is permanent; like an actual business.

Damien glanced left and right as he moved between the pallets. The harsh glare of the strip lighting above made it hard to see clearly. Shadows cast their ominous tentacles over everything and made it feel like something nasty could jump out into the light at any moment. Damien took his time and moved slow.

The way up ahead was clear, the warehouse deserted. It was eerie without the bustle of labourers and warehouse workers. It was like an empty boat drifting at sea: it made no sense without people.

Where is everybody?

There were several more doors leading off from the warehouse, but none of them were open – only the one up ahead was. Light spilled out from a corridor beyond.

Damien approached the open door and moved through it silently, his axe held high and ready. He was beginning to feel a bit like James Bond.

A one-armed, axe wielding James Bond.

Maybe James Bond's working-class cousin.

At the end of the corridor was an unlocked office. Someone was inside.

Damien bent his knees and crept along the wall. The man inside the office was facing away, rummaging through the drawers of a desk and stacking papers and folders into a pile.

Getting ready to clear out of here?

Damien snuck into the office and positioned himself behind the stranger. He raised the axe and prepared to strike a blow against the back of the other man's skull.

But he reconsidered when he saw who the man was.

Damien took a step back and spoke. "So we meet again?"

The man in black overalls spun around and almost hopped up onto the desk. There was fright in his eyes but not necessarily terror. He looked down at the axe and then up at Damien's face. "What are you doing down here?"

Damien held up the bloody stump of his arm. "Didn't you hear? One of the monkeys escaped from the zoo."

"You should have bled to death by now. You shouldn't be here. You should be in the house"

Damien couldn't help but laugh. "Seriously? Should I just go back, then? Just wait for you to kill me like a good little boy?"

The man seemed to realise the absurdity of his words. He stiffened up and seemed to get over the surprise of seeing Damien, but he was clearly still wary of the axe ready to strike him. "What's your plan then, Rambo?"

"Depends."

"On what?"

"On how much you help me. I want to know what this is all about."

"You already know."

Damien frowned. "Revenge? People have paid to have us all killed?"

The man nodded. "In a nutshell, yes."

"Who's running this thing?"

The man looked away.

Damien raised the axe threateningly.

"Okay, okay. This whole thing is run by Black Remedy. It was set up to allow people to take revenge on those who have wronged them. Bets taken on the black market just add to the profit margin and allow us to keep doing this. It's a rich man's day at the races."

Damien shook his head. "That's insane. How do Black Remedy expect to get away with it? They're a public company for Christ's sake."

The man huffed and looked at Damien like he was an idiot. "Because they've been getting away with it for decades. You think you're the first person to be here, son?"

The hair on the back of Damien's neck stood up as he thought about just how long 'decades' was and how many people could have been tortured in that time. "You people are going to burn in hell."

"So are you. You all deserve to be here. We're just giving people justice."

"And taking bets on it all. Very noble. Tell me why it looks like you're in a hurry to get out of here?"

"Because we're shutting up shop. We always do after the competition concludes. Next year we'll do the whole thing again someplace else. We only ever stay in one place for two or three years at a time. They'll be razing the place to the ground in less than an hour."

"Who will be?"

The man shrugged. "Site security."

"The men wearing the jumpers with the eyeball logos on them?"

The man nodded.

"You're in charge of them, aren't you?"

The man nodded.

"Well," said Damien. "You better hope that you're not still asleep when they start the fire."

Before the man had chance to understand, Damien whacked him with the thick head of the axe. The blow struck him in the temple and sent him sprawling back over his desk. The papers he had been gathering fell to the floor in loose piles.

Damien was glad they would soon be setting fire to this wretched place. He just needed to make sure that he wasn't inside when it happened.

32

D amien found his way up a flight of stairs and was now out of the basement and on the ground floor. There were people buzzing round in various rooms and offices and he was forced to stick to the wall like some sort of drunk, one-handed assassin.

The ironic thing was that the people on this floor were all wearing shirts and ties, milling about like ordinary office workers – except that, instead of telesales and purchasing, they were administrating the running of a death camp.

How do these people sleep at night?

Damien wanted to take his axe to every one of them, but there was no way that he could succeed in the task. He had to prioritise and, right now, that meant escape first and foremost.

The floor was set up like a typing pool, with multiple workspaces all set up with blinking computers. Disturbingly, some desks had pictures and personal effects on them too. The people here looked at photographs of their families while signing off on the deaths of innocent victims.

Well, maybe not 'innocent', but human beings at least.

Damien peered around a partition wall into a nearby cubicle and saw that its computer displayed strings of numbers which looked very much like betting odds. The whole floor must have been one giant bookmaking operation.

The main problem about escaping through it was that there were a dozen men and women all scuttling around the place like busy worker ants. Getting past them would not be easy. Damien eyed an exit up ahead, but there were several cubicles to get past first.

This is so much easier on Xbox.

A young woman with a pink neck scarf and a grey pencil skirt was bent over a desk up ahead. She was typing away at a computer, deleting files most likely. Damien watched her for a few seconds and then crawled up behind her, close enough to smell her lavender perfume.

Damien crept past the woman and slid into the next cubicle that was empty. He hid behind the partition wall and took a breather. His heart was beating like a kettle drum and each throb sent a spike of pain through his mangled wrist. He hadn't even had time to contemplate that he was now missing a hand.

I don't have much future as a carpenter if I can't hold a nail.

Damien waited until the coast was clear again and crept another few cubicles ahead. A young couple were flirting up ahead and he had to wait several minutes before they parted ways. The man headed over to the opposite side of the office, while the woman walked right past the cubicle in which Damien was hiding. The way to the exit was clear.

Time to move.

Damien sprung out of his hiding place and bumped right into a man who was kneeling down on the floor. The middle-aged office worker had been filling up a cardboard box with papers on the floor. He'd been hidden by the partition wall.

The man looked at Damien in surprise, and then shock. "Hey!" he shouted. "It's you!"

"No shit," said Damien and then smacked the man square in the jaw with the axe handle.

Everyone in the office stopped what they were doing and stared at Damien. Apparently his escape from the house had gone unnoticed as they were all terribly shocked to see him.

They're not used to having to face one of their victims. I'm not just a name on a betting form any more.

Damien realised that they really had been planning to leave him to bleed to death in the house. More fool them for not checking that the job was done.

Nobody made a move for Damien. They were merely office workers and he was a bloody, half-insane mess. They weren't about to take the risk in being the company hero. What someone did do, however, was trip an alarm.

The siren began wailing throughout the entire building. It seemed to incite the office workers as they all started to filter out through side doors and stairwells. Damien ignored them and headed for the exit he had been seeking from the beginning.

He started to jog and then sprint as he entered a carpeted hallway. It was like being in the head office of any ordinary firm. It was furnished and homely.

A door on Damien's left made him skid on his heels. He stepped back and peered through the glass pane on the door. Two people stood inside the room. One of them was a stumpy little man with a balding head and bookish spectacles. The other one was Danni.

Damien needed to escape this place before the security guards arrived. They would be planning to bury Damien on the spot or perhaps just leave him to burn when they started the fires. But, seeing as his chances for survival were so low anyway, Damien decided to change his priorities. He couldn't resist the opportunity that had just presented itself.

This place was built for revenge. Maybe it's about time that I got some of my own.

Damien turned the handle and kicked open the door. Danni and the stumpy man spun around in fright. They had both been staring at a computer screen with their backs to the door. Damien wasn't sure but it had looked like a video call with someone, but as soon as he entered the room, the window on the screen closed.

The sound of footsteps thudded down the hallway outside. Damien locked the door and hoped it bought him some time.

Danni was the first one to speak. "Damien! What the hell are you doing here?"

Damien suddenly went dizzy, but he fought it and hoped it didn't show. Whether it was the booze or his injuries, he did not know. He let the axe swing menacingly by his side as he spoke. "We promised to go out and get a drink, remember?"

Danni backed up against the computer desk. The stumpy man stood in front of her and put a hand up. "Now look here, young man, none of this was personal. If you stay calm, I'm sure that we can work something out."

"You'll have to excuse me," said Damien, "but who in the blue hell are you?"

The man cleared his throat and seemed to think. "I-I'm just a technician. I just look after the computers."

Damien smiled. "Guess this has nothing to do with you, then?"

The man smiled and nodded.

"Except," said Damien. "That you look after the computers at a building that tortures and murders people."

"Now look here!"

"No! You look here, you fat little weasel. One more word out of your maggoty lips and I chop 'em off. You get me?"

The man shut up.

Danni was still cowering up against the desk. Damien looked at her and grinned wide. He imagined he resembled some sort of deranged lunatic. The feeling was good.

He took a step towards her, draping the axe casually over his shoulder. "Oh now, what to do with you, my sweet sweet darling."

"Damien, just calm down. You sound like a mad man."

"The alternative is being a dead man, so I'm fine with having a couple screws loose. Besides, who would blame me?"

Somebody bashed a fist against the door and yelled something. It was one of the security guards outside in the hallway. Danni made a run for the door, grabbing at the handle.

Damien swung the axe at her head, but buried it in the wall only inches away. "SIT. THE. FUCK. DOWN!"

Danni backed away from the door and took a seat on a nearby swivel chair.

"Please, let us go," said the stumpy man.

Damien sniffed. "I just have a few questions first. You understand how it is, first day in the office and all. Let's think of it as an orientation."

"So ask your stupid questions, then," said Danni. There

was a look of insolence in her eyes. She did not enjoy being on the bad end of this exchange.

I hope the irony isn't lost on her.

"Well, firstly I want to know where we are. How far to the nearest civilisation?"

The stumpy man answered. "We're on the Isle of Mull. There's nowhere for miles and the only way to reach the mainland is by ferry.

Damien sighed. *I'm screwed.*

He pointed the axe at the stumpy man. "Then I need to use a phone."

"No can do. When the alarm was tripped, all outside communication was locked down. The whole place is designed to make sure you don't get out of here alive. The only mistake was assuming you were already dead. We should have kept our eye on the cameras."

"You were watching me? I thought you were just a technician."

The man's eyes widened slightly and he nodded eagerly. "Yes, yes, I am. I was working on the camera feeds when they left you to bleed to death in the kitchen. I-I can't believe you survived."

"I've survived a lot over the past ten days, so why quit now?"

Danni sniggered. She was lounging in the swivel chair now with her hands on the armrest. She seemed quite amused by it all. "You're a dead man," she said. "You'll never get out of this place alive."

The banging on the door increased and several faces appeared at the glass window pane. More security guards.

Damien sniggered back at Danni. "I wouldn't be finding it so funny if I were you. I may be screwed, but that just means I have no more fucks left to give."

Damien swung the axe without warning and brought it down on Danni's left hand which was braced against the armrest. She bellowed in agony.

Blood sprayed into the air.

Damien kicked Danni's severed hand aside as she dropped to her knees and wailed like a cat on a bonfire.

Damien stared down at her without pity. "Guess we're even."

The stumpy man slid up against the wall and looked like he was about to piss himself. There were tears forming in his eyes and his lower lip quivered.

Damien lunged at the man and grabbed him by his sweat-stained shirt collar. "You're coming with me," he said. "Time for the guided tour."

33

When the door opened, Damien came out behind the stumpy man. The sharp edge of the axe was pressed up against the man's windpipe and Damien was ready to slice it open at a moment's notice.

The half-dozen security guards had evacuated the office floor and they were now the only ones left. Damien kept them at bay by drawing a little blood with the axe.

The stumpy man bleated. "P-please, help me! He's insane."

Damien grinned. "You better bloody believe I am. I am one bloke you do not want to test right now."

The security guards kept their distance but maintained pace with Damien as he backed down the corridor with his hostage.

"How do I get out of here?" Damien asked the stumpy man.

"I-I don't know."

He drew the axe along the man's throat and drew a little more blood. "Guess again."

"The...the corridor on the right. Take the corridor coming up on your right. It leads to the car park outside."

"This goddamn place has a car park? I bet it has vending machines and water coolers too. You people are sick."

"We provide justice," he said. "A...a service."

Damien took the corridor on his right. The guards pursued him cautiously. "You sound pretty passionate to the cause for a lowly technician."

"W-we all believe in what we do. It is a *just* cause."

"Except that I'm innocent of the crimes you allege of me. I wonder how many other mistakes were made with previous contestants. I hear you've been doing this a while. How many innocent people have you killed in that time?"

"None of them were innocent. And who gave you that information?"

"Why do you care?"

"B-because I am worried who else you've managed to hurt in your escape."

Damien was nearing the end of the corridor. "The only person you need to be worrying about right now is yourself. Now, which way do I go?"

The stumpy man pointed his trembling finger. "That door, there. It leads outside."

Damien backed up against the door and shoved it open. It led to a small waiting area lit by the growing light of dawn. Everything outside the windows was dark blue, heralding the imminent arrival of the sun.

"What will I find out there?"

"Staff vehicles. That's all."

"That's all I need."

Damien kicked out and slammed the door he had come through closed. It hit one of the guards and sent the group of them back into the corridor. Damien used the brief advantage to slip out of the reception room and out onto the hard concrete outside.

It felt surreal to finally be out of the facility, away from the house. He felt like a caged sparrow suddenly being released. But he also knew that he was far from free.

The guards flooded out behind Damien and began ordering him to give himself up. Instead, Damien searched around for another option. Up ahead was a long bus, perhaps the one that had brought him there to begin with. It was full of people who looked all ready to set off.

"Who are all those people?" Damien asked his hostage while pointing at the bus.

"The benefactors."

"You mean the people who paid for us all to be here?"

"They just wanted to see justice served."

"So you gave them a front row seat?"

Damien thought about all the videos he had seen; all of the broken and damaged people looking for a way to ease their pain. As much anger as he felt, it was not directed at the people on the bus. They were victims, too, and could perhaps be excused for their bad judgement. They were not the cause of all this. They were being used no differently to the housemates. Their pain was being used as a way to profiteer. The people responsible were the ones who had turned suffering into a business.

"Where are they heading?" Damien asked.

"The ferry."

"Then I hope they go back to their lives and manage to find some peace, because this shit is over."

"Sir, I need you to release Mr Hammond and put down the axe," said one of the guards.

Damien smirked. "Mr Hammond, huh? Nice to put a name with the face."

"I'm just a technician," he said. "Let me go."

"But we're just getting to know each other."

"What would your friend, Harry, think about all of this, Damien? He would never condone you taking a man hostage, or cutting off a woman's hand."

"Danni is a lot of things, but a *woman* isn't one of them, and if you mention Harry's name again I'll cut you."

"Just let go of me and we can work something out, son. You can take the prize money and go and help your friend."

Damien hesitated for a second as something became clear. "You're not a technician are you? You know too much about me."

The stumpy man used Damien's lapse in concentration to drop to the floor like a sack of potatoes and escape his grasp.

The guards were on Damien immediately. An elbow caught him in the chin and made him see stars. He tried to hold onto the axe, but before he knew it, it had already dropped to the ground as half a dozen bodies piled on top of him.

If it were not for the whiskey dulling his senses, Damien would have probably lost consciousness; especially when his skull hit the pavement with a *clonk!*

"Get him up!" said the stumpy man who Damien now knew was The Landlord.

The guards dragged Damien up off the ground and held him in front of their boss.

"You really should have bled to death." He sneered. "It would have been easier on you."

Damien spat a mouthful of blood. "Piss off!"

The stumpy man wound up a punch and landed it against Damien's ribs. The air rushed out of him.

Two hundred yards away the bus full of 'benefactors' departed for the docks. Damien wished he were with them.

Least I got some payback against Danni. If nothing else, there's that.

"How on earth did you get into this?" Damien said. "How do you sleep at night?"

The Landlord smirked. "How do you think I got into this? Money. As for how well I sleep, well, let's just say I've never been one for sleeping anyway. It's overrated."

"So, what now? You kill me in cold blood? You got the stones for it, you fat fuck?"

"I never get my hands dirty. I just give my word and things get done. Allow me to demonstrate."

The Landlord leant in to one of his guards and whispered something. The guard nodded and then headed off. While that was happening, the other guards moved Damien further away from the building. The Landlord followed them.

Two minutes later the facility blew up.

The force of the blast was like a gale force wind. The flames lit up the dawn sky and plumes of smoke twirled in the air like billowy dancers. The air filled with ash and debris.

Damien choked and spluttered. "Jesus! Weren't your people in there?"

The Landlord shrugged. "A few. All of my permanent staff are out of the way. Those left inside were expendable. Better just to part ways with them. New project, new staff. That's the way we do things around here."

Damien huffed. "Beats severance pay, I guess."

The Landlord waved a hand dismissively. "Take him somewhere private. Bury the body."

A guard grabbed Damien from either side and dragged

him along the concrete. They steered him towards a patch of scrubland at the edge of the car park. The sun lay on the horizon ahead.

"So you couldn't just get a job at a supermarket like everybody else," Damien said as the two men dragged him by his arms.

"Shut up," said the guard on his left.

"No, seriously. Why do this?"

"Because it pays better than working at a supermarket."

Damien's feet left the concrete as it gave way to mud and grass. He knew there were only seconds left until the two men killed him.

But he wasn't out of ideas yet.

For the last few yards, Damien had gone limp and weak, acting as if he were already a beaten man. The guards either side of him held on to him tightly. Too tightly.

Suddenly, Damien sprung backwards on his heels and broke free of the men's grasp. Immediately they spun around and came after him.

Damien was ready with the chef's knife hidden behind his belt. He slid it out and pointed it forward. The nearest guard ran right into it.

Damien pushed the knife deeper into the guard's belly and pulled him into a tight hug, using the man's body as a shield against his colleague. Then Damien pushed the wounded guard backwards and sent him colliding into his friend.

The two guards fell to the floor, one bleeding on top of the other. Damien swung his leg and kicked the uninjured man in the face, cleaning his clock and knocking him cold. The other guard bled out on top of him.

Damien knelt down and wiped the bloody knife against the dead guard's jumper. Then he stood up, turned around, and stared back at the flaming remains of the facility.

With the sun behind him, Damien was hidden in shadow. He used that fact to his advantage as he studied his surroundings. There were still a few handfuls of personnel loitering around the area, but most were getting into a fleet of black Range Rovers and driving away, completing their mass exodus. The Landlord was amongst them, talking on a phone and ordering people around.

Damien cut a wide arc, heading as close to the flaming remains of the facility as he could stand. The very air itself was heated and it was like walking through a sauna. Hopefully the constant shifting of the fires would mask his own movement, but he kept low and moved quickly.

Once he made it over to the nearest Range Rover, Damien crouched down beside one of the large 21" rims. He peered around the back of the vehicle and watched as more personnel departed. As each one left, Damien's odds increased.

They're making the mistake of assuming I'm dead again. They really need to get better at this.

Somebody was coming.

Damien looked left and right and saw nowhere to go that would not leave him exposed. He reached up and grabbed at the handle of the Range Rover's rear passenger door. It was unlocked.

He pulled the door ajar and slid inside the vehicle, squeezing down into the spacious foot well and making sure he was out of sight. Then he hooked his trainer inside the door's armrest and pulled it shut again.

Two seconds later, the driver's door opened and a body jumped behind the wheel. The vehicle rocked back and forth on its springs and then settled.

The front passenger door opened and somebody had brief conversation with whoever was in driver's seat. They spoke about 'cases' and the driver said to 'leave them with me.'

Then the engine grumbled to life.

Then the Range Rover started moving.

Lying in the foot well, Damien had a seductive desire to go to sleep. He had been through so much and his body was wrecked and his mind was begging for downtime. What he wanted more than anything else in the world right now was a soft bed someplace safe.

But not just yet.

Damien sprang up from the foot well and sat up on the back seat. He quickly leant forward and placed his knife against the driver's throat. When he saw it was The Landlord, he could not believe his luck.

"Well well well, looks like I caught the right taxi."

The Landlord's eyes went wide and then settled on the rear view mirror. The fear in his expression was clear and it gave Damien a satisfied grin.

The Range Rover started to slow down. Damien dug the knife into The Landlord's throat. "Slow down and you die."

"What are you going to do?"

Damien eyed the two suitcases on the front passenger seat and saw what was inside them. "I'm going to have a little revenge of my own," he said, staring down at the millions in cash. "Then I'm going to take my winnings. Just keep driving."

The Range Rover switched off its lights and cut through the hills, heading in the opposite direction to the other vehicles. Damien kept smiling at all the money on the front seat and then at the terrified expression on The Landlord's face.

Maybe things were going to work out after all. Harry was going to get his procedure...

And The Landlord is going to get what's coming to him.

Looks like I win, thought Damien as he watched the sun rise beyond the hills.

"We still can't get a fix on The Landlord, Mr Raymeady. It looks like maybe he went off the grid with the money instead of giving everybody their cut."

Samuel Raymeady looked up from his mahogany desk and studied his employee with his dark, smouldering eyes. "No matter," he said. "In a few days, the money won't even matter. There are much greater things ahead of us. It's time to see some real change in the world. The time for punishing worthless sinners, one soul at a time, is over. It's time to take a larger approach."

"What do you mean, sir?"

Samuel smiled, his snake-like incisors glinting in the orange glow of his office lamp. On his desk lay a vast sheet of paper. It was the blueprint for a cruise liner that his company, Black Remedy, owned: The *Spirit of Kirkpatrick*. "You'll see," he said, folding his hands on top of his desk. "You'll see very soon."

WANT FREE BOOKS?

Don't miss out on your FREE Iain Rob Wright horror starter pack. Five free bestselling horror novels sent straight to your inbox. No strings attached.

For more information just visit the website:
www.iainrobwright.com

PLEA FROM THE AUTHOR

Hey, Reader. So you got to the end of my book. I hope that means you enjoyed it. Whether or not you did, I would just like to thank you for giving me your valuable time to try and entertain you. I am truly blessed to have such a fulfilling job, but I only have that job because of people like you; people kind enough to give my books a chance and spend their hard-earned money buying them. For that I am eternally grateful.

If you would like to find out more about my other books then please visit my website for full details. You can find it at:

www.iainrobwright.com.

Also feel free to contact me on Facebook, Twitter, or email (all details on the website), as I would love to hear from you.

If you enjoyed this book and would like to help, then you could think about leaving a review on Amazon, Goodreads, or anywhere else that readers visit. The most important part of how well a book sells is how many positive reviews it has, so if you leave me one then you are directly helping me to continue on this journey as a fulltime writer. Thanks in advance to anyone who does. It means a lot.

MORE HORROR BOOKS FROM IAIN ROB WRIGHT

- Escape!
- Dark Ride
- 12 Steps
- The Room Upstairs
- Animal Kingdom
- AZ of Horror
- Sam
- ASBO
- The Final Winter
- The Housemates
- Sea Sick
- Ravage
- Savage
- The Picture Frame
- TAR
- House Beneath the Bridge
- The Peeling
- Blood on the bar

OTHER BOOKS IN THE HELL ON EARTH SERIES

- The Gates (Book 1)
- Legion (Book 2)
- Extinction (Book 3)
- Defiance (Book 4)
- Resurgence (Book 5)
- Rebirth (Book 6)

Iain Rob Wright is one of the UK's most successful horror and suspense writers, with novels including the critically acclaimed, THE FINAL WINTER; the disturbing bestseller, ASBO; and the wicked screamfest, THE HOUSEMATES.

His work is currently being adapted for graphic novels, audio books, and foreign audiences. He is an active member of the Horror Writer Association and a massive animal lover.

www.iainrobwright.com
FEAR ON EVERY PAGE

For more information
www.iainrobwright.com
iain.robert.wright@hotmail.co.uk

CPSIA information can be obtained
at www.ICGtesting.com
Printed in the USA
FSHW010039271221
87194FS